# *Prescriptions*
# FOR BOREDOM

*Take Two a Day*

ALSO BY RUTH ADA CLARK

*Beauty in Bent Grass*

# *Prescriptions* FOR BOREDOM

## *Take Two a Day*

*Ruth Ada Clark*

 **VANTAGE**Press

Published by Vantage Press, Inc.
419 Park Ave. South, New York, NY 10016

Manufactured in the United States of America
ISBN: 978-0533-165087

Library of Congress Catalog Card No: 2011913361

0  9  8  7  6  5  4  3  2  1

The author would like to express appreciation to the Dubuque Country Historical Society and National Mississippi River and Aquarium Archives for historical data.

Of the thirty-six short stories printed here, only sixteen are pure fiction, the rest historically accurate. But then, truth is stranger than fiction, and it's hard to differentiate between the two.

—Ruth Ada Clark

# Prescriptions

# *Prescriptions*
# FOR BOREDOM

## *Take Two a Day*

# Old Soldier's Cemetery

GREAT GRANDMA CELIE's farm was where I thought it should be, barely visible down the lane from the deserted roadway. Overgrown fields of grass and wild flowers concealed it but the matriarch of all elm trees beckoned with its branches, saying, "Could I find the little farmhouse it had been sheltering all these years."

"Great Gran Celie!" I shouted as I ran to the house. No answer. The kitchen porch was a shambles, the door yawning open, the inside a disaster area. Chickens had taken over the place to roost. There were droppings and feathers everywhere, but evidently the cats had chased and caught them in a grand free-for-all. Furniture was knocked over, everything tumbled in heaps. No sound, no sign of life, no food in the pantry. I turned on the tap. The ghost of a sigh emitted from the rusted pipe.

I tiptoed into the tumbled-about dining room whispering, "Great Gran Celie, where are you?" A horrible thought electrified me into opening the hall door and dashing up the narrow stairs to the two tiny bedrooms tucked into the attic. Wisps of curtain let in the sun to reveal empty beds. At least she hadn't died in her sleep. But where was she?

Apprehensive, I descended the stairs. Opening the parlor door, I peeked into the hushed dark. Curtains were always kept shut lest sun fade the carpet. "It's like she's keeping it for some important person, or for some dead body to be laid out for viewing," my father had always said. I drew the heavy drapes aside. No one was there. Only a musty mohair davenport and chairs, her piano, her knick-knack shelves, and one fine cherry wood rocker on a braided rug. *George Washington at Trenton* gazed out sternly from his gilt frame at a paper calendar reproduction of *Girl With Cherries* hung opposite him, her smile enticing.

"At least you're not laid out in your own parlor," I mused fingering two china dogs and a porcelain soldier I'd never been allowed to touch as a youngster. Great Gran Celie would seat us in the parlor when father brought us to visit. After five minutes of small talk she'd say, "Come sit in the dining room while I bake sugar cookies," and she'd close the curtains and parlor door behind us. Unlike the parlor standing ready for mourning, Great Grandma Celie LeFlambeau always graced her table with flowers or a bowl of fruit. Her dining room was as cheery as was she. She kept her pine wood floors scrubbed and her kerosene lanterns polished. Not that she didn't have electricity, but she thought she was saving it. When Great Grandpa Pierre LeFlambeau died, Grandpa Claude put a generator into the pump house so she could have running water and electricity, but Great Gran kept the windmill, just in case. Framed in the window, its veins bled rust atop its lithe legs. The silence recalled the pulsed thrum of the generator, a comforting mechanical purr for me on summer nights that not infrequently puttered into sudden quiet, the stillness summoning us sleepers in our nightclothes to the dark pump house to wake the nodding golem. Water supply and lights depended on that steady grunting sound.

When Grandpa Claude and Grandma Lily died in a car crash, my parents had already moved to Oklahoma. While father was at work in the oil fields one day my mother, Sylvia LeFlambeau, died in a kitchen fire. My father, John White, an orphan, treasured his LeFlambeau connection and brought me back each summer to visit Great Gran Celie after she was alone. He tried to persuade her to come live with us in Oklahoma. She insisted, "I told Pierre seventy years ago that I'd never move again. This is my home. I intend to stay here until I'm one hundred." And she had. Or had she? Tears welled up in my eyes. "Oh, Celie, have you gone to the hospital? Are you in a nursing home? I must find you!"

Quietly closing the parlor door, I walked through the jumbled dining room to wipe a layer of dust from her favorite picture of Florence Nightingale, the *Lady with the Lamp*.

"She was so gentle and so good to the soldiers," Great Gran used to whisper with a faraway look in her pale blue eyes.

"Tell me about the war," I'd beg. "What did you do?" I'd feel in her apron pocket for the round metal ball she always kept there. She'd lay it in my palm and roll it around saying, "I helped dig this out of a soldier's leg. I helped Miss Nightingale. I carried water, I. . . . " That long ago and terrible war still troubled her. She'd only been five or six. Her face would cloud over. Quickly she'd put the ball as thick as your thumb back into her pocket. "I don't want to talk about it. Let's go make sugar cookies." Over the years she'd grown pudding plump from her great need to sugarcoat her haunting childhood.

Fleeing from the horror of war, Pierre and Celie had worked their passage to America scrubbing clothes and decks. They'd worked their way through the Pennsylvania oil fields, then Ohio, Indiana, and Illinois husking corn, digging potatoes, planting peanuts, picking and drying tobacco, saving what they could. Finally they'd settled here in Cranberry, Wisconsin, and worked the bogs while living in a sod hut dug into the sandbank. They'd built up their farm house above them. They grew into their town. Folks called her a faith healer, a saint, sent for her to sit beside their sick beds. She'd hold their hands and their breathing would ease. When someone had died Great Gran would sit at her piano with Great Grandpa beside her rehearsing duets they could sing at the funeral. Pierre was a fine baritone, and Celie had a high sweet voice with an unusually rapid buzz of a vibrato to it, shiny bright as a Brillo pad.

Times turned hard and Pierre lost much of his farm. He became bitter. He was in the fields by four in the morning; Celie would have pork chops, mashed potatoes, and apple pie ready by six and clang on the brass bell on the porch to call him to breakfast. Pierre would spit tobacco juice on her floor. Celie never said a word, but pushed the spitoon closer. When he'd eaten, she'd scrub the floor again, an uneasy truce between them. Then the bull gored Pierre. Though she nursed him tenderly, he died. Celie took the clapper out of the bell, gently wrapped it in a napkin and put it far back in the silverware drawer. "Pierre won't be answering our call anymore," she sighed.

My father hated to leave Great Gran Celie alone but was

working hard in Oklahoma to send me to college. The last time we'd visited she'd lost a lot of weight and had taken to wearing Pierre's pants and shirts. "Makes more sense with me doing the farm work, and I hate to see them go to waste," she said as she lit her corncob pipe. Celie and Pierre had always grown and dried a little tobacco for themselves and smoked pipes to keep the flies off while picking cranberries and blueberries.

"Now, Celie, you have to write a will so we'll know what to do when the time comes for you to leave the farm," said father.

"I don't know anything about wills, and I'm not leaving my farm," protested Great Gran.

Patiently he took a clean paper from an envelope, handed her a pen, and said, "Just write *I, Celie LeFlambeau, being of sound mind,*" but she wrote *I, WW LeFlambeau* and queried, "Who's going to make anything out of that?"

"What's with the *I, W W LeFlambeau* ?" father asked.

"That's my name. Winifred Wilhelmina LeFlambeau."

"Then why did Pierre call you Celie? I thought it meant Celia or Celine or some such."

She stared into the distance whispering, "Celie was someone he once loved." She took from her pants pocket a roll of money. "Here's my bank account, $790. I won't spend it so it's all yours someday." She firmly wrapped the envelope around the roll of money and circled it tightly with a rubber band before pocketing it again.

What did we really know about Great Gran Celie who'd been so traumatized by a terrible war in childhood, she couldn't or wouldn't mention it? She couldn't have been more than five or six, and now must be one hundred. After that last visit, my father died in an accident at the wells. I went off to California and worked my way through four years at Stanford. Now had I come back too late? Hurrying into the kitchen, I yanked open the drawer, found the old clapper, and put it into my pocket. I looked one last time at the forlorn mess and then crept down the cellar steps to the original basement, her summer kitchen where she'd done all her canning. "Right! Now let's find you, Celie!"

"Aha! Here's where you've been living?" Maybe the stairs had gotten to be too much for her. There were dishes on the counter and a makeshift bed in the corner, but no Celie. I hurried into the yard where the old wagon stood empty and the horse trough dry. Had the horse broken loose and jumped the fence in search of better fare? The goat she kept tied to the front post to keep the grass cropped was long gone. I found the chewed end of his rope.

"Maybe someone in town will know what happened." I drove to Cranberry, but Cranberry was no more. The General Store, Postal and Telephone Exchange building was boarded up, collapsing within. The old Creamery was crumbling to dust. Everything else was torn down, falling apart, or carted away. Driving on, I mumbled to myself to stave off creeping panic. I came to a fresh ribbon of cement. A new town had sprung up on the other side. Pulling into the parking lot of the first grocery store in sight, I entered and asked a clerk, "Where's Cranberry?"

"Produce aisle, second on the right," he offered smiling.

"No, I mean the town of Cranberry."

"Oh. When the highway came through, they drained the swamps. That was the last of the cranberry bogs. I guess the town just picked up and moved here where commerce is good."

"Well, do you know where my grandmother Celie LeFlambeau might have gone?"

"Don't know about any Celie, but LeFlambeau rings a bell. That's where that old soldier was from, used to come in here often to sell his cranberries. Blueberries, too."

"That was my Great Grandmother Celia LeFlambeau."

"No, he was a man. Smoked a pipe. Didn't say much. Drove an old wagon. Bought sugar and flour, that's all. They found him, you know, in a ditch, couple of springs ago. Town felt real bad. Nobody even knew his name. But we're real proud of him. He was an old soldier from World War One, sort of an unknown soldier."

"That was my Grandmother and it was the Crimean War!"

"Couldn't have been. He had a musket ball in his pants pocket, and a roll of money wrapped in an envelope that said First World War, LeFlambeau. That's in France, you know."

"Well, what happened to her?"

"Him! County did him up real proud. His body was all decomposed from lying in the ditch all winter. Maybe a car bumped him off in a snowstorm. Anyway, they put him in a box and buried him in a little cemetery up the hill. Used his money to build a fence around it and put up a fine monument for him. He's the only old soldier we have so he's quite an attraction. The County plans to make a county park out of that piece of land with nature trails for hiking and biking. Took it for back taxes, you know."

Tears choked me. I turned away, unable to reply. I knew whereof he spoke. There was a tiny family burial ground at the farthest edge of Great Gran's property. I found it just as the clerk had described it. A new fence with an arched sign over it read OLD SOLDIER'S CEMETERY.

I slowly walked onto the freshly cut grass. The first marker was broken and faded but I knew it read PIERRE LE FLAMBEAU, GREAT GRANDPA. Next was a marker simply reading LILY AND CLAUDE, then a row of nine little white stones like pillows marking infants I'd never known. Then I reached the big shiny marble monument engraved, "HERE LIES THE BRAVE UNKNOWN SOLDIER. FIRST WORLD WAR, LE FLAMBEAU, FRANCE."

"Oh, Great Gran, I'm so sorry!" I cried. "I didn't even sing a song for your funeral." I wiped my tears from the top of the monument and, with my pen knife, carved into it WINIFRED WILHELMENA LE FLAMBEAU. "It means torch, flame," I told her. "Your family has been all about death and dying, but you're not. You've been all about life and living. You carried the torch the best you could for as long as you could. I'm proud to be your grandchild and I'll try to be like you. They made a lot of mistakes on your monument, but *brave unknown soldier*, they got that right."

As the years pass by I still come here to Great Gran's grave. I bring flowers to lay at her monument, but never find it bare. The townspeople or school children, or perhaps families who've lost a loved one to war, bring field daisies or violets, lilies of the valley or trillium. I always find little bouquets. They never forget their brave, unknown, old soldier.

# The Crazies

AND THE RAINS came. Thunder clumped over the distant mountains determinedly dumping skies full of rain until the hill streams overflowed, coming down in sweeping torrents to engulf our town. Our town, which liked to pretend it was a city, within hours became a floating sea. The cobblestone streets were awash with our fishing boats, loose fence posts, carts, firewood, squawking ducks, flapping geese, and struggling cats and dogs. Our hundred shops and houses all held hands, stone wall to stone wall, lining the narrow streets. Nowhere for water to go but up.

And the rains continued. It seemed harmless at first, flood inching up our stoops and playfully splashing at our doors, but then it boldly seeped across our floors, gushing and pushing and shoving into every room. It rose, grabbing and swirling anything unattached back outdoors. It filled our homes with smells of forest, mud, fish, and river water. We were used to floods. Folks simply carried what they could up to their second floors and let the river water have its way. Straw brooms, wooden stools, empty crocks all floated outside into the muddy waters to collect in little groups like gossips huddling to hear the news.

I made quick coins at first rowing townspeople back and forth as they tried to carry on with their business. By now each house stood knee-deep in water, doors flapping in the current, doorways half-full and drowning, windows brim-full and weeping. The butcher hung his ham hocks and sausages in his upstairs window. The merchant piled his wares on his balcony. Rope ladders were strung from upper stories to their owners' boats below as trade went on. The Matron Manotti looked wistfully over her balcony rail. A railing floating by gave me an idea.

"I'll see what I can do for you," I called up to her. "Be back later." In my boathouse I nailed a platform onto my boat. With a long enough pole I could punt it along by pushing against the submerged cobblestones. Next I fashioned another smaller platform fenced all around with sailcloth so no one could fall out. I fastened it to a pulley raised up on my tallest mast. The rope I strung on a winding drum with a ratchet wheel to control slow raising and lowering. Out into the flooded streets I pushed my boat.

"My good man," cried the Matron Manotti importantly swishing her hips, "Here are some coins if you'll just take me to the shops and back." Without ado, she lifted her layers of billowing skirts to clamber over her balcony railing and into my teetering elevated platform box. My sweat poured down with every pound of her I lowered to my boat. At the butcher's and baker's I achingly repeated the process of raising and lowering her in my elevator box, then took her home.

"Now be sure to come back for me tonight at seven. They plan to give the operetta in the town hall attic. There are plenty of storage boxes for everyone to find a seat."

"Don't you know there's more rain up in those mountains?" I protested. "We'll all be flooded out by morning! You're crazy putting on an operetta! All of you are crazy if you don't pack up and get out of town!"

"What? Leave my lovely house and beautiful town? You're the one who's crazy! Every generation of your Otis family has been crazy. Not a clever thought in one of your heads, and you're no exception! Your children and all of the Otis grandchildren will probably be crazy, too!"

# Harmony

INSIDE PANDEMONIUM REIGNED, but there was peace out here within the yellow clay brick walls of our extensive compound. I loved this garden pond where gently swaying weeping willow fronds trailed against the water's surface. A miniature deer stood stock-still behind a tiny maple thinking I didn't see him in the shadows. Farther along in the sunny waters a stilt-legged crane silently watched for unwary goldfish. I leaned over the pond rim closest to the house and gazed at my reflection in the pond as my maid spread my freshly washed hair across my shoulders to dry. She buttoned my slender silk sheath all the way up to my neck. Combing and parting my hair, she braided one side.

"Now go and help with the wedding preparations," I told her. "I want to braid the other side myself." The blazing sun made the water a perfect mirror as I looped my long braid into several coils to hang low over my left ear fastened with a slender bamboo stick. I picked a fresh pink water lily to add to my braids, then began to plait the other side. The top must remain smooth, leaving plenty of room to balance the three-tiered pillowbox silk wedding crown.

My eagerly awaited bridegroom would wear the matching crown. Smiling, I pictured just what he was doing now. As all the warlords did when riding home from battle, he would cross the last river, turn in his saddle to throw down upon the bank his leather helmet, breastplate, gauntlets and greaves, then dash himself and his saddle to the ground. He and his horse would jump back into the river to swim awhile, washing away all the dust and sweat from the clothes he wore, from his gleaming black hair, and from his horse. Then he would clamber onto the bank to dry in baking sunshine. Saddling up, he would tie his armor to the saddle and remount to ride, hair and main whipping in the fresh breeze. Sedately would my rugged, handsome young lord enter town and approach our gateway.

Winter had seen our parents making a contract, spring had seen payment of the dowry, and summer now brought the three priests to receive the offering and perform the marriage. Since early morning nosy neighbors and noisy relatives had streamed in bearing flowers, bowls of fruit, cloth-wrapped gifts, all determined to not miss any of the festive preparations.

"Ahhh," they all sighed as the ancient scrolls inscribed with "LONG LIFE," "GOOD FORTUNE," "PEACE," and "HARMONY" were hung, one on each wall.

"*Mmmmm,*" they all murmured as the delicious aroma of cooking sweetmeats wafted from behind the screened-off kitchen area.

"*Ohhh,*" they all exclaimed as the matching pale yellow heavy satin bride's and groom's robes with blue and jet black beads were draped over a low couch, and the matching white three-tiered wedding crowns encrusted with pearls and jangling jet beads were displayed on the piles of cushions awaiting us. Loud had been the squabbles until at length it was agreed the wedding robes would be lent from the groom's ancestral keepsakes and the crowns from the bride's family, to be worn for the ceremony and then carefully replaced in the red leather trunks until the next wedding.

The sharp rap of a cane at the garden gate woke me from my reverie. "Can someone see who is beating with that stick?" I called, but my parents and the servants were too busy to hear. With hair half braided, I opened the gate myself. "What do you want, Old One?"

Only a toothless grin from a scruffy beggar in gray-green rags greeted me in reply. His mustache and beard straggled in thin whisps, tufts of white above each ear rimming his bald head.

"Are you hungry? Come with me." I led him into the great hall and told the servants, "No one should go hungry on such a happy day. Take this old grandfather to the kitchen for food."

"For shame!" called out the neighbors. "The eldest in the house deserves the best seat." So my parents showed him to a soft stool at the head of the long, low table. He lifted from a water bowl a lighted floating candle and held it to the edge of his clothing which burst into flames. We all shoved him down and rolled him on the floor, smothering the flaming rags to ashes.

"Why did you do that?" I snapped, stamping my pretty little slipper at him. Only a toothless grin answered as he stood in his sooty loincloth.

"For shame!" called out the neighbors. "This old grandfather is trying to show you he is ashamed of his miserable clothing at this celebration." So my mother sent servants to fetch one of father's finest robes to clothe him. Next he started crawling around on all fours.

"Get up off the floor, you stupid man," I demanded. Only a toothless grin yawned back at me.

"For shame!" proclaimed all the neighbors. "This old grandfather wants to play with the grandchildren." So my parents handed down the kites and string. They sent the old man and the younger children tumbling out into the garden to play.

"He may be too old to talk but he is a clever fellow," said all the neighbors. Busily we rearranged cushions and stools around the table and set the room to rights. Behind our backs the old man shinnied up the doorpost and fastened the kite string to the upper corner of the panel screen, slid back down and yanked hard. The entire panel came out of its sliding track to crash down upon guests and table, exposing a kitchen full of astonished servants.

How propitious a moment for my bridegroom to arrive at our main gate, hand his horse's reins to a servant, and be shown into the great hall! Bowing low to the assemblage, he raised a politely blank, almost stern face, struggling to show no puzzlement at this most paradoxical wedding reception. Relatives held the old man fast while servants struggled to reassemble the wall panel. Mother scurried to pick up broken bits of porcelain. Father righted the table. Neighbors dusted me off.

"It was not our fault," chorused the neighbors. "This bride has been disrespectful to her old grandfather!"

Shyly I approached my lord, explaining, "He's not my grandfather. He's just an old beggar who knocked at our gate."

For a second there glinted from the corner of his dark eyes that which I love about him, a sparkle of amusement and understanding, but quickly he forced his face into a stern mask. Gruffly he demanded of the old man, "What have you to say for yourself?"

Only a toothless, foolish grin replied.

"This old man should be caged up where he's safe. He doesn't know what he's doing," pronounced my lord. "Send for the authorities."

"For shame!" shouted all the neighbors. "Would you send him to prison at his age? He may be too old to speak, but he really has a clever mind."

"What good is a clever mind if you cannot direct it to good use? He no doubt escaped from confinement. No matter where he is, he will always be a prisoner of his own mind. Send for the authorities."

"Aha," nodded all the neighbors. "Your bridegroom is not only brave, and strong, and handsome. He is also wise!"

# Spitting Image

THESE TWO GUYS are Gadney and Trout all over again, the red head and the blond, and entering the Police Academy just like us, only different, somehow, and better, more equal in size, voice, and personality.

You have to understand how it was with Gadney and me. It was Doughboy and Spike behind our backs, or Mutt and Jeff. As plain-clothes detectives we were a very good team for over ten years. A perfect bad cop, good cop pair, Gadney was loud, brash, and pushy. His temper about to explode, he'd nervously pop a cigar in and out of his mouth, then angrily jab it at the stubborn, silent suspect.

"Now, Clyde," I'd calmly interject. "Put away the cigar. You're trying to quit, remember?"

"Thanks, Oliver." He'd smooth his wavy red hair, pocket his cigar, and beam his wide open smile. Relieved at the sudden change, the suspect would spill before another angry outburst from Gadney. They always responded to that smile. We all did. A boyish, innocent, and expansive smile, fresh and ready. Even his freckles seemed friendly.

Did Gadney's smile ever win over the girls! They'd do anything for him, hang on his every word. I was more or less invisible to them.

It happened the season we joined the dramatic society. When you work ten-hour shifts six days on, two off, six on, two off, you need something to keep you from going crazy. We'd started as backstage crew shifting scenery, handling curtains, lights, and sound effects. That's how we met Violet, a sweet pretty blonde young thing holding the prompter's job at curtain side. Violet was quick, accurate, organized, and helpful. She'd copy into her prompter's book the director's every suggestion to remind the actors later if needed.

"How did we decide that entrance worked best last time?" called out the director.

"Enter up left door while still looking backward," Violet called out quickly. After I missed several light and sound cues, Violet took to whispering, "Lamp up, spot out, knock off left," or whatever was coming up next. I stayed close, quite close, to Violet. Like lavender, she smelled. Violet's lips parted softly, ready to whisper cues. Her long lashes curled gently against her cheeks. She was a valentine silhouette there in the dark by the curtain. Oh, yes, I stayed very close to Violet.

Gadney had started going down in front and demanding changes and improvements. With that big booming voice he soon took over from the director. They all accepted it because he was usually right, a quick study of people, and knew what looked natural or didn't. Lucky for us Gadney knew every line because the play opened for a Friday and Saturday run, but the lead broke his ankle tripping after the last curtain call Friday night. Gadney took over the part Saturday with flair—he played himself, not the character, but it worked. He won over the audience with all his boyish charm, and the curtain fell to raucous applause.

I'd made up my mind to ask Violet out afterward and reached for her hand. Violet looked up at me expectantly.

"Keep your hands off that little lady," boomed Gadney, bursting backstage. "I've had my eye on her for some time and I'm taking her home." All the girls were gushing around him and Violet melted. Off they went.

Gadney took her to his house, sat her down on the sofa and poured out his life story: wife dead four years, children seventeen down to five years, no mother's love. He was lonely. They were like two lost puppies. They rejoiced at having found each other. They ended up in his bedroom.

Morning brought a radiance to Violet's smile as they descended the stairs to whip up a family breakfast. After the first bite Gadney held fast to the table edge. In a gray tone he finally said, "Let's go out on the porch for some fresh air." Miracles do occur.

Reverend Fontain was just strolling by the house. "Come over here, Reverend Fontain, I need you. I want you to marry us."

"Why, of course, Clyde. When do you want the wedding?"

"Right now, and start with the 'Do you take' bit right away." The urgency in his voice made the Reverend comply. As soon as the vows were repeated and man and wife pronounced, Gadney sank down on the porch steps, leaned against the railing, and never moved again.

"Call the Doctor! Call an ambulance!" Violet shouted at the few neighbors who'd gathered at the strange goings on. Violet quietly herded the children back into the house and made them sit, zombie-like, at their breakfast. They'd gone to bed with a

father and no mother. They awakened to a step-mother and no
father.

Gadney wasn't buried in uniform. Undercover officer's identi-
ties are never advertised. We wore business suits and our hearts
on our sleeves for a man we'd all loved. Violet was her usual organized, efficient self until I showed up. She rushed into my arms
and we sobbed. The force was appalled at our unseemly display
of emotion. Violet and I sank to our knees, bowing our heads.

"Help us understand what's best," she continued. Our tears
were under control now. We stood up still clinging to each other.
Suddenly the force understood about Violet and me. They gathered around us at Gadney's graveside.

Violet took the next nine months in stride. She quit her job
and became a full-time mother. She organized the household
responsibilities, convinced the youngsters they enjoyed putting
their bikes and wagons, skates and buggies away safely in the
garage each night. She convinced them they enjoyed doing the
yard work together, and enjoyed showing her off at school, at
church, and at the grocery store.

When Gerald Gadney was born, he had his father's gorgeous
red hair and lovable smile.

Now I suppose you want to know about Terry Trout. I tried to
help out the family as much as I could. I tore down the wretched
trellis over the front sidewalk. The flowering climbers had been
mangled and boards splintered by child climbers. I widened the
driveway. Violet painted bias stripes so she and the teenagers could
each park yet back out without blocking the other. Months passed.

"You're all invited to a wedding Sunday," I announced to the
force.

"What took you so long? We've been expecting it," they laughed. In another nine months Terrance Trout was born, blond and beautiful.

Gerry and Terry have grown up, close as brothers can be. Terry grew fast and soon evenly matched Gerry. They did everything together, football, basketball, chorus and band. Gerry was calmer than Gadney ever was, and more helpful and easygoing. Terry was less shy than I, more eager to reach out and to speak up. Now they're entering Police Academy together and it's like Gadney and Trout all over again, the red head and the blond. When I say spitting image, I mean it's their personalities that are so much alike. They're the spitting image of their mother.

# Chicken Light

RELUCTANTLY HIS COLLEGE enrollment forms were signed and turned in. Reluctantly his grades were maintained and graduation achieved. Wearily his last night on the job as Hotel Campion bellhop was finished.

"Now remember, you promised me," Tom said. "I get the whole summer off to myself."

"What do you want to do?" Imagining both Tom and sixteen-year-old Sylvia would ask for a vacation trip to Atlantic City, I'd been squirreling away every spare cent from my part-time job as saleslady at LaLique.

"Ray and I are going to camp out at the old park by the pump house."

"There's nothing there but broken down seawall and sand." The once beautiful lake had been drained and turned into productive cornfields. Overgrown bushes and trees hid the former park entrance leading back into the wooded hillside. "You won't even find restrooms there anymore."

"So, we'll go behind the wall and cover it up with sand. Nobody comes by there anyway."

Now it was my turn to be reluctant. I drove Tom and Ray up the weed-choked road until stopped by a fallen log. They jumped out eagerly, with little more in their knapsacks than a jacket, some sliced boloney, and a loaf of bread each.

"You can't live on that! And what will you do if it rains?" I knew Tom had regularly banked each paycheck.

"We'll be fine, Mom. Just drive by every fourth day at first light with a package of bologna and two loaves of bread. We'll be right by this log sleeping."

"Well, then, Sylvia, what do you want to do this summer?" I asked my daughter.

"I want to work at LaLique like you."

Surprisingly freed from household care, I took the full-time position offered to me as head of the ladies department and Sylvia came along.

"What's she doing here?" the manager asked.

"She's my assistant to lift and carry. I intend to inventory and rearrange the entire department," I replied. Sylvia loved being amid all the glamorous clothing, though we ourselves wore only plain white blouses and black skirts. By week's end they'd hired Sylvia full-time for all her usefulness. She bought nylons and under-things with her first paycheck, but then started a savings account toward college.

I wondered if Tom might lose sight of college. When I drove up every four days with fresh bread and sliced bologna, he'd be sitting on that log slipping into his battered old felt-lined rubber boots. But it had to be early or they'd be nowhere in sight. Where did they go and what did they do, I'd ask. Nothing and nowhere were the usual replies. Never a word outside of "Nothing" and

"Nowhere" were the usual replies, and never a word out of Ray. But they seemed alright. Did they sit on a log and wait for the rare lunar moth or sapphire blue to flit by? Did they try to figure out what kind of hopscotch the little green toads were playing? When Sundays rolled around I'd ask if they'd like to come into town for church or to spend the day. A shake of their heads was the only reply. When I worried about vitamins Tom said, "Fruit grows on trees, Mom. Staff of life." He stashed the loaves of bread in his knapsack.

"But it's getting so hot this meat will spoil."

Ray then uttered the only words I heard out of him all summer. "We eat that first."

Meanwhile, with money saved from the aborted Atlantic City trip, I bought a new car, well, not new, but new for me. Green, and I loved it. We'd park second from the alley corner at a two-hour meter, and every two hours dependable Sylvia would duck out the back to insert another quarter just before the meter maid pounced with a ticket. They met so often they became friends. Sylvia was a real winner in the ladies department. She was slender and youthful. When a customer was undecided about a dress, I'd say, "Would you like this young clerk to model it for you?" Sylvia had an eye for color and style. She never wore jewelry herself, but quickly could select just the right combination of earrings, shoes, handbag, or gloves as she hurried into the fitting room. She'd emerge aglow with confidence wearing the entire ensemble with such pleasure the customer would say, "It's perfect! I'll take it, accessories and all." Did they imagine themselves looking as young and glamorous as Sylvia?

Tom changed a bit over the summer. I wondered how many

nearby towns they'd hiked to. Tom and Ray both had sturdy work shoes I didn't recognize. Occasionally they were wearing clean but worn work shirts I'd never seen. Had they been pitied by some local mission, or had they hired out as day laborers for farm work or road crew? They became deeply tanned, taller, more muscular. Maybe they'd climbed trees. Once I arrived to see Tom's cheek and throat deeply scratched.

"Have you been fighting with wildcats!?" I shouted.

Tom calmed me down with, "I washed it and it's okay. I forgot rule number two."

"What's rule number two?"

"If you have to go to the bathroom in the dark of night, try to take somebody with you."

"What's rule number one?"

"Don't waste any chicken light," and they disappeared into the woods.

I felt guilty that my daughter and I were having such fun at LaLique, but Tom and Ray seemed happy. Maybe they just needed time away from us women.

Last week of August finally arrived. I drove to the woods with some trepidation to remind Tom it was time for college. He smiled and looked down at me. I could swear he'd grown a foot. "I'll need some new clothes," he said woefully, staring at his worn, knee-length jeans. But they were clean. He and Ray had surely enjoyed every swimming hole for miles around. They tumbled willingly into the car.

When next I led Tom out of LaLique, it was with a mother's swollen pride. He had a complete new outfit from the men's haberdashery. We drove to college and entered the Administrator's office.

"Well, young man, what have you been doing all summer?" asked the Administrator.

Tom reached forward to shake hands and said, "I didn't waste any chicken light, sir."

It had to be a man thing.

# Who Was
# Mrs. Santa Claus?

CHRISTMAS CAME ON Wednesday that year. Snow had already blanketed the sooty world's sins with gracious beauty and heightened anticipation of after-school sleigh riding for the little ones. Uncle Oscar owned three terraces down from Seminary (now called Clarke Drive) to Lowell, which provided gardens, orchards, chicken coop, rabbit hutch, bee hives, and room for play and experimentation for his fun-loving brood, eight of his own children and three adopted kids from Hillcrest Baby Fold. He brought home cardboard boxes from the Herrmann Furniture Store for his kids attending Jackson School to use sliding down the Foye Street steps which were never shoveled early in the morning. Aunt Bertha now hugged and shooed them off to school that Monday, December 23rd, some toward Jefferson Junior High, but the rest toward Senior and Jackson Schools. We cousins always hurried to walk with them.

"John, see that they all watch at the crossings. David, take Jimmy and Richie's hands in case it's slippery," Aunt Bertha called after the boisterous group. Monday was her busy day. She shut the door to her hall entrance and straightened her favorite pictures there. On one side was a red plush framed quotation in gold embroidery from Joshua, "As for me and my house, we shall worship the Lord." On the opposite wall hung a framed Madonna, a black mother tenderly holding baby Jesus. These two hangings let everyone entering her house know where she stood on these issues.

Bertha sailed into the kitchen, and I do mean that literally. Bertha needed a wide berth. She was tall, wide, and bountifully endowed, with high piles of hair just showing silvery streaks. Bertha began her constant, cheerful, trilling, Bing-Crosby-eat-your-heart-out whistling. Her friends called her Birdie for good reason. She bustled about clearing the breakfast dishes and bread pans to soak in the sink, storing the extra bread in the cupboard. Her large family required setting bread every night to rise and baking it fresh early each morning.

Next Bertha hurried to the basement to start the first load of laundry which the four girls on Monday mornings dutifully collected from upstairs bedrooms and carried to the basement for her. Turning the boys' pockets inside out before washing, she emptied from Jimmy's a folded note.

"Oh, no, Jimmy! How careless of you!" She read the note.

"In order to clear the stage for rehearsal, there will be no afternoon Kindergarten Class Monday, Dec. 23rd. Parents may bring the Kindergartners back in time for the Christmas Program Monday from 2 to 4 p.m. The P.T.A. Ladies will provide refreshments for parents, and Santa Claus will bring treats for the students."

"That's in six hours!" Panic struck. Bertha hurried upstairs, raised the phone receiver, and asked the operator to connect her to Red 218. "Hello, Ada, did you get a note from school? We have to take refreshments for parents today at 2 o'clock. I just found Jimmy's note. What can we do? I thought I had everything taken care of with all the treats already delivered." Having students in so many grades, Bertha was President of Senior, Jefferson, and Jackson School P.T.A.s simultaneously. She had ordered candy canes for every student in 7th through 12th grades. For the past two weeks she'd had us girl cousins under Mama Ada's direction sewing six-inch cheese cloth bags with yarn draw strings for Santa to fill with treats and pass out at Jackson Grade School. Mama explained that Santa had appointed Grace, Marjorie, and me as helpers because he had so many children to think about, which impressed and satisfied us. Bertha had busied her own children popping popcorn and storing it in tins until last Saturday. The bigger children over the weekend had secretly filled the bags with popcorn and hard candy, and Uncle Arthur had already delivered them in his truck to Jackson.

"I'll make two angel food cakes," volunteered Ada. "If you make two, that should cover it. Surely no more than forty-eight parents will show up. I suppose Richie lost his note."

They both hung up their phone receivers and set about separating their two dozen eggs for the angel foods, whipping them with such determination the whites eagerly expanded into glistening white froth. They carefully folded in sugar and flour, and poured it into tube pans which barely fit side by side in their ovens. One hour to bake. Aunt Bertha hurried to the basement to finish washing. She had a new modern Voss washer with two tubs and a wringer, which could swing from wash tub to rinse tub to laundry basket. She sorted clothes while running water into each tub. She started the agitator for the first load of shirts, pinafores, and blouses. Then she rushed upstairs to peek at her cakes. Her modern porcelain-doored oven had no time or temperature controls, but had to be hand set and watched. Back downstairs she went to wring the first load into rinse water and start the second load of coloreds. Rinsing and wringing out the first load, she hung them to dry on the lines stretched across the basement ceiling. Second load into the rinse and third load into the washer, Bertha rushed upstairs to set potatoes boiling for lunchtime soup for the children who had an hour and a half to walk home, eat lunch, and walk back to school. By ten-thirty the cakes were out of the oven and cooling upside down over vinegar bottles. Downstairs to change another wash load. Upstairs to peel the hot potatoes, chop them to start simmering in water and milk soup to which she added a chopped onion, some peas, and a few bits of chopped slab bacon. Bertha carefully knifed her cakes out of their pans onto platters. She decided to drizzle red and green powdered sugar frosting over them. Carefully she put one on the dining room buffet, and the other on the telephone stool right beside it, out of the way of her thundering herd. The kids arrived home for lunch, stamping, hanging their wraps, and clambering upstairs to wash up. Down they tumbled again to sit expectantly at the kitchen table where Bertha ladled out soup and said the blessing. With a smile she watched their angelic heads bent over the steaming lunch. She stood in the doorway, lifted the phone receiver off its hook, and asked for Red 218 again. "Hello, Ada, how are your cakes coming? OH! NO! NO! NO!" She had absentmindedly sat down upon the telephone stool. "My cake! I sat on my cake! Ohhhh!"

"Don't cry, Birdie. It will be alright. There's time to bake another," said Ada.

"But I have only six eggs left!"

"Well, Birdie, why not try a sponge cake roll? Separate those six whites, and add to the yolks the six left from your first batch of cakes. If you spread it thin on a cookie sheet it will bake in twenty minutes."

Aunt Bertha slammed the receiver onto its hook. The kids realized this commotion would not be helped by laughter. They piled their dishes into soapy water in the sink, rinsed them, and stacked them quickly on the drainboard, then quietly grabbed their wraps and headed back to school.

"Mama, you will come to the Christmas program, won't you?" called Adele from the doorway.

"Yes, dear," answered Bertha while trying to scrape frosting off the seat of her dress. Muttering, "This is all your fault," to Jimmy, she led him upstairs. "You play quietly in your room and stay clean until time to go to the school program. I must change my dress and I have work to do."

In a whirlwind Birdie re-entered her kitchen to whip her egg whites with such a vengeance that they snapped to attention in obedient peaks. Combining the rest of the ingredients, she gently spread the batter on a wide cookie sheet and started it baking. She ran to the basement to resume the continuous washday process. Running upstairs she luckily found her cake just done. Turning it out on a clean dishtowel, she rolled it firmly and placed it on the back doorstep for quick cooling. She mixed more red and green frosting, fetched and unrolled the sponge cake onto a platter. Slapping red frosting all over it, she firmly re-rolled it and fastened it with two toothpicks. Artfully she frosted the outside of the cake roll with green, and then sifted a drift of snowy powdered sugar across the top. "My, my, it's as Christmassy as can be, better than I'd hoped." She put this platter and a sharp knife into a large picnic basket, and the one good angel food cake in a regular metal cake carrier.

"Jimmy, come down now. It's time to catch the bus," she called while donning her hat and coat. She stuffed him into wraps and headed outdoors. The Seminary Hill bus stopped exactly in front of Bertha and Oscar's house. Mama Ada was already waiting with Richie and two cakes. They climbed aboard and Jimmy, who didn't really understand why but knew he was in the doghouse, sat meekly between them and their cakes. Transfers were needed to get to Jackson School. They got off at Senior High and the West Locust bus met them in a very few minutes to whisk them down to Jackson.

"Well, the timing worked out right, and your sponge cake looks perfect, Birdie," said Mama, peeking under the basket covering. They crowded into the auditorium with the rest of the parents.

Mrs. Frieda Stoller's kindergarten class usually met on the stage, but today their little chairs were lined up for them in the front row of the auditorium with bigger children in the next rows, and adults in the back. Even Mrs. Stoller's desk had been moved to the cloakroom. The front window curtains were drawn to darken the stage, except for the floor footlights. Mrs. Stoller was a smiley, lovable, round little woman. Children from 5th and 6th hinted to kindergarteners that she might really be Mrs. Santa Claus. We very much doubted that as we'd seen Mr. Stoller, a thin little dried up apple core of a man.

Kindergarteners stood and faced the audience to sing *Jingle Bells* in their chirpy childish tones. First graders filed on stage and sang *Away in a Manger*. As the Principal helped the first graders down, and the second graders filed up onto the stage, she said to the audience, "In this program we honor the birth of Jesus. What special lady do we also honor?"

Jimmy piped up, "My Mother! She's a lady!"

The Principal said doubtfully, "Do you even know what a lady is, child?"

Jimmy turned to beam at his mother, saying earnestly, "Well, she always wears white gloves, and she has lace curtains in her windows." Everyone laughed and clapped at the obvious love shining in his face. The program continued. At the end, a roly-poly Santa in a red plush suit with white fur came laughing onto the stage and passed out treat bags to all with pats on the head and hugs around the shoulders. Parents enjoyed their cake served on paper plates, the very latest invention of the 20th century.

"Weren't these cakes finger-licking good!" declared Mama as they rode home on the bus with Jimmy and Richie. Aunt Bertha hugged Jimmy close, saying, "Your class was the very best and I'm so proud of you." She kissed the top of his head. The rest of us trudged on home, seriously debating whether that was really Santa Claus, or Mr. Stoller with padding, or Mrs. Stoller who could borrow Santa's suit because she really was Mrs. Santa Claus.

# Mystery in
# the Deep Woods

NO MONEY CHANGED hands, just real estate, an unorthodox way of moving. When Pete and Pamela retired from years of two-hour twice-a-day commuting on California's eight-lane highways of bumper to bumper traffic, it was to the peace and quiet of Nicolet National Forest on Scattering Rice Lake in Northern Wisconsin. They didn't even pick the place. It was thrust upon them. A voice at a retirement party whispered, "Here's a number you should call." Pete called.

"I don't want to buy or sell, but exchange properties, and soon," said a stranger's voice on the phone. Pete flew to Wisconsin to inspect the property and fell in love with miles of tall pines, homes scattered few and far between around the lakeshores, the nearest town small but sufficient to support tourist trade summer and winter. The house was a modern ranch design, its basement full of storage cupboards and freezers for food and supplies to outlast winter storms. There was a small tractor-mower-snow-plow combination in the garage to manage the long front lane and diminutive space of grass, a deer-feeding stand in full view of the living room windows, the nearest neighboring houses barely visible beyond deep woods on all sides. Pete returned to California ecstatic over the gorgeous sunrise-dappled lake, the thick hush of pines so tall you had to look straight up to glimpse the moon and the stars. Oaks, maples, shrubs and grasses crowded between to add splashes of color everywhere. Pamela called the movers and began to pack. They drove cross-country at a leisurely pace, allowing the movers a chance to arrive before them.

"Hello, you there!" Sprightly redheads met them at the door. "We're the Ribleys in the house on your left with the totem pole in our lane. We run the drugstore in town. Here's your house key."

"And how are you? You come a long way," from a swarthy couple with dark hair and foreign accent. "We the Strovados, house on right. We run *Lavender Lady*. Come to eat. We open every day at eleven and at four."

"So glad we found this place. We're retired from California," replied Pete and Pamela. "Since you're here, how about helping us shift the heavier furniture to where it looks best?" After pushing and shoving sofas and tables, the neighbors left them amid boxes to be unpacked.

"What do you think?" Pete asked hesitantly.

"Give me a chance to take it all in. I'd like to look around first," Pamela answered. Hand in hand, they went from room to room finding all the fittings clean and new to the point of luxury. Touring the outside, they found concrete steps with iron railings. They went down several landings through overhanging pines and woods, at last reaching a small clearing at their shoreline with a dock stretching out above pebble-bottomed water. Their speedboat floated at its dock with connecting walkway. A hand-pushed lawnmower leaned against a locked equipment shed, which left just enough tiny yard for a picnic blanket to be spread. Friendly ducks gabbled, wobbling on and off the shoreline as if awaiting their handout.

"I didn't expect all this!" Pam said and they both smiled at their good fortune. Climbing back to their new home, they found a uniformed Ranger in their yard.

"Bureau of Land Management" he announced. "We manage the forest and lakes hereabouts. You need this brochure telling you what you can and can't do. Preserving everything just as it is must be your first concern. Fires only in well-cared for and tended indoor fireplaces. No trees or shrubs cut. No downed wood on your land collected without permission. Downed trees on the shoreline must be left where they fall into the water as a natural habitat for fish and wildlife. You may feed the deer in winter at your stand, but we don't advise it. They're wild animals. They may attract bear. The bears will stay in the deep woods across the road. You stay on your side of the road nearest the lake. If you see bear markings on a tree, it will be three straight claw scratches higher than a man's head. Just stay inside and call us. We try to move the bears deeper into the woods. No animal or bird may be caught or killed. See the sheriff about a fishing license. No speeding on the lake—it ruins the shoreline. All trash must be driven to the dump south of town. It's kept permanently burning in a pit that keeps the bears away. Any questions?"

"No, and we'll obey all your rules," volunteered Pete shaking hands with the Ranger.

"And I thought California had its worries," laughed Pamela.

"We made our little Japanese gardener sad if we let any of the plantings in the atrium die, but at least he didn't eat us. And all we had to do to keep the peace in the neighborhood was to hire the young Jewish boy on the left to water them in the morning, and the little African American boy on the right for the afternoon watering."

"Ma'am, you're in Wisconsin on federal land!" With a curt nod, the Ranger walked stiffly away.

"That was more warning than welcoming," muttered Pete as they went inside.

Wonder upon wonder greeted them as Nature's handiwork took them into close embrace. Wildflowers hid at tree bases, orchids peeked from hillside greenery, loons called across the lake at dusk and dawn, the eagle screamed and spiraled on high, leaping bass splattered rings on the sunlit waters, sighing winds played the topmost pine branches like harp strings, squirrels, chipmunk, raccoon, possum all ventured near their house softly rustling about, but deer approached in total silence after dark. Fall was colorful and noisy with birds at their busiest. Several bird feeders had to be hung to tone down the squabbles over food. Winter brought hush and better visibility as leaves fell and snow filled the space between tree trunks.

"I can see a bit of light. It must be the Strovados' house there," Pam observed, peering from her darkened living room out into the night to watch the deer gathering at the stand to munch corn. Next day it was, "A second big black van is parked over at the Strovados' house. All the men who got out were bundled in black."

"Forget about them now," interrupted Pete. "Tell me what

you think of Tony. They recommended him to call out every time there was a heavy snowfall to shovel off our roof. I saw him in the barbershop and he agreed to come, but he told me he'd have to have cash, no checks. He wouldn't even tell me his last name. Should I hire him?"

"Sounds shady or criminal to me," said Pam. Then she squealed, "Oh, what if we've landed right in the middle of the Mob, the Mafia, you know, like the Bonano Family!"

"Sounds more like the man who traded this house for ours," said Pete calmly. "He didn't want any names on paper or any checks exchanged, either. I thought it was probably the witness protection program avoiding putting things in writing. Besides, the Strovados' name isn't Italian, more Middle European. The *Lavender Lady* did strike me as an odd name for a restaurant, though, since the whole restaurant is done up as a Wisconsin hunting lodge with those deer and fish trophies and all the wood paneling."

Pamela returned to literally spying on her neighbors from the dark. Next morning Pete took his turn watching and called, "Pam, come quick! Something's going on." Men in dark jump suits could barely be seen through the dense woods rushing, tumbling, and bumbling up and down, then disappearing down the hill toward the lake. Their coming and going and muted calls and commands kept up until noon, when they all got into their vans and drove off.

"Could they be terrorists?" whispered Pam. She and Pete spent the day in worried musing. By late afternoon the vans were back and the same rigmarole started again until dusk.

"Should I call the sheriff?" Pete wondered. "Maybe I should just wander over friendly neighbor fashion and see up close."

"Don't go! Don't go!" cried Pam. "I'm afraid. I don't like spying, but let's wait and see." Morning brought flashes of bright orange suiting with blue and green helmets on the men dashing about through the trees. There were loud shouts and cheers as the drill continued with flashes down the hillside and out onto the lake ice, then dashing back uphill.

"Terrorists don't wear orange," stated Pete. "Put on your wraps. We'll go act like nosey neighbors."

With great good humor their neighbor, Mr. Strovados, greeted them saying proudly, "You see our four-man bobsled team practicing their takeoffs? We invite them come get in good shape. They off soon to rent practice time on real bobsled track. They wear colors of our flag. Get ready for Olympics. Only team from Azerbaijan!"

# Uncle Walter and
# the Elephant's Behind

AUNT MATTIE PHONED from Beetown, "Can you take your Cousin Walter off my hands for awhile?"

"What would I do with him?" hesitated Mama.

"Well, couldn't you use someone to wallpaper and paint at your house?"

"Is his leg healed enough for him to climb ladders?" asked Mama.

Mattie replied, "Oh, yes, he's been on top of the silo and fixing things up all over the farm. It's just that when his friend Jack Daniels is around, that bull makes straight for him again."

"Well, we don't let Jack Daniels or Demon Rum in this house. Maybe a visit to Dubuque would do him good. I'll have Henry phone you tonight if he agrees." Mama hung up the receiver and asked, "Would you like a visit from your Uncle Walter?"

We jumped up and down excitedly. Uncle Walter was a roly-poly potato sack of a man who always wore Osh Kosh bib overalls with a big red handkerchief dangling from his side pocket. We couldn't figure out why that tame bull of his had backed Uncle Walt up against the side of the barn, breaking his leg. That bull was so tame Uncle Walt could lead it around by its nose ring. Last summer he'd even seated all four of us kids on the bull's back and had Aunt Mattie take a snapshot. The broken leg must have all been the fault of that Jack Daniels and Demon Rum, whoever they were.

"If Papa will let Uncle Walt come, we'll lock his friends out," said Richie, who was all of four years old. I was six and Margie and Grace were eight and ten. We said we'd double up in beds to make room for him.

When Papa came home from the furniture store he agreed, "Both this house and my brick apartment house need attention. I won't have him in this house but he can stay in that lower apartment. It's empty now and I won't rent it until he's finished a few things for me."

What a disappointment to Richie and me! We only got to see Uncle Walt on weekends. He'd come for picnics in our backyard. He'd help us wash our fox terrier, Jiggs, in the large tin wash bucket. Richie and I could barely turn the cistern handle to make water trickle from the spout, but Walt could effortlessly fill the tub in a flash to overflowing. We got to suds and rinse him and Margie and Grace had the job of wrapping Jigs in towels and hanging onto him until he was dry. Only when he was rid of fleas was Jiggs allowed into the house. Then Uncle Walt would blow on the rinse water so my brother and I could race the little boats he whittled for us. Uncle Walt laughed uproariously as he read the funny papers to us. He enjoyed the *Maggie and Jiggs, Little Orphan Annie, Boots and her Buddies, Barney Google, Ella Cinders,*

*Popeye and Wimpy,* and especially the ridiculously complicated inventions of *Rube Goldberg*. Uncle Walt would walk us down North Main hill to Henry Torrey's Grocery on Kaufman Avenue and Valeria Street. After thumping and "plugging" watermelons for ripeness under Mr. Torrey's frown, he'd buy the juiciest and lug it back uphill for our supper. Then he went on up to the brick apartment where he was on the lower floor, Aunt Grace was on the upper, and another family rented the main floor.

Uncle Walter busily painted all the outdoor Colonial columns, porch banisters, window and door trims white. The top moldings, slanting inward from both sides to a center hollowed out scroll, took time. Next Papa started him on indoor woodwork. Grace and Margie were old enough to walk uphill daily to help him move chairs, carry paint buckets, arrange drop cloths, enjoy his company. All we got to do was stay home and collect the *Little Dutch Boy* emblems he cut from all the paint cans and sent to us. One weekend he took us kids on the streetcar to enjoy Eagle Point Park wading pool. He even took us fishing down at the Mississippi River boat ramp on Fourth Street.

Aunt Grace had Walter paint her bathroom and kitchen. "For a farmer used to slapping paint over a whole barn in one day, he's surprisingly neat, even artistic," she phoned to say. "He used spring green for my kitchen table and chairs, even edging the little knobs and rims in orange and black." Next thing she was phoning to shout, "Walt's fallen off the wagon! You'll have to get him out of here. I can't stand him another minute!"

When Papa came home, Mama broke the news, "Walt made so many trips to the paint store he's run into his old friend Jack and fallen off the wagon." Richie and I wondered why this Daniels fellow would push his old friend off a wagon, and whose wagon was it, anyway?

Papa said, "Perhaps we could bring him over here and put him to wallpapering. I'll bring home some wallpaper rolls tomorrow." We jumped with delight that Uncle Walt was moving here. Papa brought home paint and paper to keep him busy. Walt papered the dining and living rooms. Then he painted the kitchen a cream color and used a sponge to stipple a spring green haze all over it. Entrancing! The bathroom he painted lavender, using cream and green sponges to stipple an overlay. Magical!

Uncle Walter offered to take us down to Jessie's Junk Shop on Central Avenue. Mama, who was busy giving piano lessons, agreed. We went from our North Main backyard across the field where Heeb and Shelby Streets were never put through because they failed to line up. Lengthy cement steps descended to Central about where the A & P Store was. Uncle Walt left us at Jessie's Junk Shop, saying he had to see a man about a dog but would be back soon. We spent hours gazing at penny candy through the glass showcases. Stiff tan marshmallows shaped like peanuts, fragrant yellow shaped like bananas, or fluffed pink like ice cream piled on top of triangles of waffle cone were our favorites. Richie finally bought three painted tin fish with a little horseshoe magnet strung from a short bamboo fishing pole. I bought tiny black and white scottie dogs mounted on magnets with opposing charges so they would push or pull one another depending on which way you turned them. When Walt finally returned, we trudged home to meet Mama's fury. "I know where you've been! How dare you leave my children alone!" When Papa came home, she declared, "Walter's visit is over!"

"Not just yet, Ada. I've brought some very special paper for

Ruthie and Richie's bedroom. I need him to put it up. Walt, I've measured closely and it will just cover. Start to the right of the doorway so, if you run out, use some plain paper over the door-frame where it won't be noticed."

We both helped clear our room so he could start next day. Uncle Walt's method was to place chairs around the room and walk on one after another as he hung strips. First he cut a two-foot piece and pasted it above the doorway. Next he set up two ironing boards. He measured to the ceiling and began unrolling the paper upside down on the ironing boards, cutting each strip, and laying one on top of another ready to be slathered with paste and hung. We huddled in the doorway, fascinated as large circus animals in pastel gray, pink, and blue unfurled from the roll on cream-colored background. Horses pranced, seals balanced balls. A ballerina stood on one toe atop an elephant's neck, but her leg was floating off somewhere else. Strange! I noticed in odd places around the room I could read by little dotted red lines *Cut Here*. Richie put his finger on a gray blob asking, "What's this?"

"That's the elephant's behind," said Uncle Walt.

"If that's his behind, where's his before?" persisted Richie.

Uncle Walter stood back, looked, and finally said, "Up here's his before. See his trunk? Pretend it's a puzzle. Every time you find an elephant's behind, follow the seam up until you find his front half." He took from his pants pocket a flat bottle of brown liquid and drank from it. He finished the room hurriedly, drank the rest of his bottle, sprawled on the floor and snored loudly. Mama came to investigate, then sadly led us away.

When Papa came home that night, Mama sent him to view the scene. We watched as Papa, a rather formal little man who never raised his voice but never was at a loss for words, turned beet red. Silently he walked straight downstairs to telephone Aunt Mattie in Beetown, Wisconsin.

"Walter wants to come home," he said loudly into the mouthpiece.

"When should I drive down to pick him up?"

Papa shouted into the phone loudly enough for everyone in Wisconsin to hear, "NOW!"

# Legend of
# Little Fleet Foot

MANY AGES PAST when Old Man Mississippi was just a wandering brook, he came from out the North to settle down among these hills. With him came the Red Man, the strong and silent Red Man, to climb these rocky ledges, roam these woodlands, stroll these grasslands.

The oldest Indians watched the council fires. The strongest braves used bow and arrow to hunt the forest creatures. The young men speared the catfish in the creeks.

Now, the littlest Indian of all was Little Fleet Foot. He really couldn't do much, but he loved to lean against the birch and watch the soaring eagle, or leap the running brook, or race the bounding hare. One day Fleet Foot sat on a boulder by a raspberry thicket eating juicy wild berries. Old Wise Bear came lumbering along.

"Oho, Little Fleet foot," rumbled Wise Bear, "Why do you sit lazily picking fruit? Don't you know the creeks are running dry, the catfish are disappearing, and soon we'll have nothing to eat!"

"Aha, Little Fleet Foot," said Busy Squirrel hurrying by. He stopped long enough to add, "Take warning! Move on. The leaves are withering on the trees, the springs are drying up in the ground, and soon this land will be nothing but dust!"

"Whooo knows where to find a better place?" said Great Horned Owl, poking his head out the front door of his tree home. "What if all the waters under the sun be drying up, and all the land be dying?" He closed his eyes and slowly shook his head.

Fleet Foot trembled like a silver poplar leaf. He cried, "I must hurry back to my teepee and tell my father, Whistling Wings. Maybe the big chiefs in the council ring will know what to do." He was off in a rush of wind. Sprinting along the homeward trail, Fleet Foot saw the sun falling below the treetops, darkening the woods with pink and purple shadows. As he rounded the bend, the muffled sound of drums and shuffle of moccasined feet was heard. He darted between the teepees to his own.

"My son," said Whistling Wings standing just inside the tent flap, "see the council fire smoke rising in the dusk and know that great trouble is upon us. Tonight we dance to the thunder drums and burn offerings to the Spirit of Waters."

"Will that help?" asked Fleet Foot.

"I don't believe so," sighed Whistling Wings as he carefully adjusted his feathered wrist and ankle bands.

"Is there nothing wiser to do?" asked Patient Doe, mother of Fleet Foot, rising from her woven mat.

"Only the Great Spirit, himself, would know," said Whistling Wings softly stepping out to join the big chiefs.

"I am much too small to help them," said Fleet Foot, "but I can run to the Great Spirit for help."

Fear clutched at the breast of Patient Doe, but she only smiled and fetched a pouch of dried beans and deer meat to hang upon his shoulder. Then she took off her shell beads and placed them round his neck, saying, "Take great care, my son, and hurry. I will be waiting for you."

Out into the dark slipped Little Fleet Foot to silently dash down the trail. All night long he ran until, at first wink of dawn, he reached the shores of the Mississippi. Kneeling there, Little Fleet Foot panted, "Mighty Mississippi, come now to my aid! Tell me where to find the Great Spirit."

"Run away," laughed Mississippi. "I am busy building a dam to hold back my waters!"

"Why do you do that now?" cried out Fleet Foot. "My people have need of water."

Mighty Mississippi only laughed louder. "Well, they shan't have mine! I had thought to grow wide and fat lying in this bed, but see how thin and weak I have become? Now I must build a dam and save my water for another day. You'll have to go to Great Spirit to find more." He was having a great struggle holding back his water and finally wheedled, "Give me your hands to build this dam and I will tell you where to find Great Spirit."

Now Little Fleet Foot did not want to part with his hands, but he was sorry to see the river struggling thus. He knew he was too little to win an argument, so he agreed. Then Mighty Mississippi said, "Run to the Wind. She'll tell you where to find Great Spirit."

Up stood Fleet Foot and dashed into the morning. Toward noon he ran over a hill and in the valley found the Wind. "Dancing Wind, come now to my aid," called Fleet Foot breathlessly. "Tell me where to find Great Spirit." She did not hear him for she was weeping and tearing her hair, lashing herself against cutting stone cliffs and huddling in valley hollows to sob and to moan. "Oh Wind, why do you weep here?" Fleet Foot cried out. "Come where my people are to do your weeping, for they have need of your water."

"Can you not tell how my skirt hems are caught in the thorns of these bushes?" she complained. "Do but give me your eyes that I might see my way out of here. You may be sure I will soar high and never dance close to the ground again to have cause for such weeping. Oh, please, little boy, and I will tell you where Great Spirit is."

Little Fleet Foot did not want to part with his eyes, but he was sorry to see Dancing Wind so torn and tearful. He knew he was too little to outwit her, so agreed. Gleefully Dancing Wind whirled off, shouting, "Run to the Clouds. They will tell you where to find Great Spirit."

Bounding off blindly, Little Fleet Foot ran and ran up and up, until at last, on the other side of morning, he felt on his cheek the cool moisture of the clouds. "Lovely Clouds," he called out desperately, "come now to my aid! Tell me where to find Great Spirit."

"Can't you see we're stuck?" pouted the Clouds, busily puffing and pushing, lugging and straining to get over the mountain peak. "We've grown too fat and lazy to make this hill, though we huff and sweat."

"Why don't you lighten yourselves by letting down your water for my people? They need your help," said Fleet Foot.

"Little one, we plan to sail straight on across the land once we've topped this mountain. We can't spare a drop or all is lost.

Oh, do lend us your feet that we may be running along," fussed and fumed the Clouds. "Then we'll tell you where Great Spirit can be found."

Fleet Foot did not want to give up his feet, but he was sorry to hear the Clouds fretting so. He knew he was too young to persuade them, so he agreed. At once the Clouds ran off. Slowly Little Fleet Foot gathered up what was left of himself, sadly struggling on. When night came he wandered into the woods. "Oh, how can I ever find you, Great Spirit!" he cried, and there before him was Great Spirit sitting on a log mending a raven's broken wing.

"Come sit beside me," said Great Spirit, lifting Fleet Foot onto the log. "Rest a bit and tell me all about it." So Little Fleet Foot told Great Spirit all.

"I have just the thing to soothe all these troubles, Little Fleet Foot, and you shall be the one to carry it home, this cool, sweet rain." Little Fleet foot rose gratefully and Great Spirit said, "Call again, any time. I'm always around."

"There's not enough of me left to finish my task," said Little Fleet Foot, stooping and trying to pick up the rain.

"That's plenty, my child," the Great Spirit replied, "for now I give you a new place to run and to play. The land between the raindrops is all yours."

Now, this Indian legend is true. Anytime you feel the cool breeze coming in before the rain, listen closely and you'll hear the pitter patter of tiny feet to prove it. That's Little Fleet Foot dashing, bounding, hurrying the good gift home.

# Why Does Aunt Kay Keep Dying?

CARRIE COLLINGS WAS a dream of a seamstress, able to create just the right dress for any occasion.

"I need a simple gown for induction as Worthy Matron of the Eastern Star," said Mama.

"I'll make you an exquisite gown!" enthused Carrie.

"No! A simple gown," protested Mama.

"A simply elegant gown?" asked Carrie, turning Mama around hopefully.

"No. A simple dress," was Mama's adamant reply.

"Very well, an elegantly simple gown," Carrie smiled at her satisfactory solution.

Carrie was white-haired and petite, a cheerful lady with sparkly rimless glasses, a lady we children loved to hug, except in the places where she bristled with straight pins between her lips, or stuck into her shoulder sleeves, and into the purple velvet pin cushions elastic-banded to her wrists.

"You girls move your dollhouses into the hall so Carrie and I can use my sewing machine," said Mama. I kept my dollhouse on top of the closed up treadle sewing machine table at the dining room window. When Mama wanted to sew, she'd lift the lid to one side and raise the machine up to sewing position.

Marjorie's dollhouse was on a card table. It was huge and had been a wonderful surprise Papa made for her one Christmas. Earlier he had taken Mama, Grace, and Marjorie to the Chicago World Exposition of 1936. Being a furniture dealer, his eye was caught by the boxed sets of rooms of dollhouse furniture. Papa bought Marjorie a brown fuzzy-surfaced living room set—sofa, chair, and ottoman; real walnut table, chairs, and china cupboard for the dining room; then tiny pewter plates, cups, saucers, spoons, and tea service. The four- and five-inch furniture pieces required a large dollhouse. Papa made it secretly in the basement and painted it a cool gray, like the latest design cement brick house models he'd seen at the Chicago Fair. It had a flat top and a roof garden on one side surrounded by thin black metal railings. Papa trimmed the house in tan and hinged one entire wall to swing open for easy access.

Aunt Rosalie had bought for me a much smaller doll house with furniture made by Tinkertoy, which was a composition of metals; a bright red sofa and piano bench, a black grand piano with a lid that opened up, a tall lamp stand with red shade, twin beds, a kitchen sink, a toilet whose seat really raised, and a tub and wash stand with brassy spigots.

Marjorie and I scavenged the house for diminutive boxes to use for footstools and end tables, glass beads big enough to look like vases, cardboard to build furniture, bits of cloth to make curtains, and shiny paper for wall mirrors. Marjorie planted tiny branches in medicine cups she painted like terra cotta pots for her roof garden, and saved bright little Japanese tissue paper umbrellas from some birthday party for when Aunt Kay came to visit for shade.

Aunt Kay was medium-sized china of the Kewpie doll variety with wavy hair painted silver, sold at all five-and-dime stores. Because her legs were solid together and unjointed, she could stand. Her arms were wired on and movable so we made doll clothes to cover her fat tummy. Though she was too big for my furniture and too small for Marjorie's, she blithely traded visits between our two dollhouses.

"Carrie and I are going shopping for dress material," Mama announced.

"Will you buy us another Aunt Kay?" Marjorie and I both begged.

"What happened to the last Aunt Kay I bought you?"

"She died," said Marjorie solemnly.

"What from?"

"She broke her leg."

"Can't your father play doctor and glue her together?"

"Uh-uh. She broke her neck, too, falling off the roof garden."

Mama looked askance at Marjorie. "What happened to the first Aunt Kay I bought you girls?"

"She died at my house," I piped up. "I think she had a tummy ache. We had a funeral for her, remember?"

Mama gave us an inscrutable look that we returned with wide-eyed innocence. Why couldn't parents accept our answers as we accepted theirs? We didn't question when they said our beloved Grandma Campbell had died of angina, whatever that was. Nor why she had lain there releasing groans with every breath. She had

always bustled hurriedly about. Then she could no longer climb
the steps. Next she couldn't make her bed, then even get out of bed.
She couldn't make us her delicious version of pizza, a frying pan
full of melted cheese poured onto a biscuit crust and topped with
her hot chili sauce. They did explain as she lay in her coffin beside
the parlor door, that she was cold and stiff because she died. They
said as we watched dirt being shoveled onto her coffin, "Don't
worry. Grandma isn't in the ground. She's gone to Heaven."

But in our silence and in our whispers, we children struggled
to understand these statements we'd already accepted from
grownups.

I had our first Aunt Kay die at my house so we could have
a funeral. We put her into a fat and fragrant pine wood pencil
box lined with a silk hanky. We put a pansy in beside her and
slid the lid shut. Grace and Adele dug a hole for her at the base
of Papa's favorite linden tree. We invited Mama, Louise, and
Mrs. Zimmerman to put aside their work and attend. I sang *Jesus
Wants Me For a Sunbeam,* Marjorie prayed *Now I Lay Me Down
To Sleep,* and we all sang *Jesus Loves Me This I Know.* Then we
served milk and crackers.

Many days later after a good rain, we dug Aunt Kay up to see
if she'd gone to heaven. Much to our dismay, she was still lying
in her box, now slimy and filled with clay. We must have done
something wrong. We covered up our mistake.

Now we clamored around Mama for a new Aunt Kay. Marjorie
had decided the second Aunt Kay had died at her house.

"You girls clear your things from the dining room table so
Carrie and I can cut the pattern there."

Grace and Adele were the brainy ones, and way beyond

dollhouses. In the upper classes at Jackson Grade School, they were fascinated by Geography. Arriving home from school they loved to sit down at opposite ends of our big table with pencil and paper to draw from memory whatever country they studied that day. Soon they'd come to the table's center chairs and open Geography books to compare papers to the map and judge whose came closest. Mrs. Buetell, their Principal, encouraged extreme competitiveness and learning with awards.

Mama always kept our dining room table extended with two leaves. Underneath, Richie set up an oval track where he and Robert sat in the center running their Lionel trains around. We all had to get out of the way when Carrie trundled in with her armload of white silk crepe to spread across the table and cut her pattern.

While they'd been shopping we'd scurried to find a pretty box for the second Aunt Kay's coffin. Tiptoeing into Mama's bedroom, peeking into her dresser drawers, we found a beautiful big silver Evening in Paris gift box of toiletries Papa had given Mama. We gazed at midnight blue plush lining and blue glass perfume vials with tassel tops.

"This round silver powder box is just big enough and the blue puff is sooo soft!" said Marjorie. Most of the powder was used up so I dumped the remainder in the waste basket. We hurried to install Aunt Kay in her resting place and bury her before Mama's return.

"Did you buy us an Aunt Kay?" we danced around Mama.

"Yes, but why does Aunt Kay keep dying? I'm going to save this one until you can tell me." Mama firmly shut her purse.

We returned to an upstairs bedroom to think on that.

One day our dog, Jiggs, killed a squirrel. We used its burial as an excuse to dig up the last Aunt Kay and peek at her condition. Another soggy mess!

"You've dug three holes at my linden tree roots. You'll make it die!" Papa scolded. "Don't do it again! Pick up the linden berries for me instead." He liked to steep the little yellow-green twin-stemmed berries in hot water to make the linden berry tea he said was good for whatever ailed you.

Then Mr. McGrath next door died. The whole town turned out. He was helping construct the shaft at Roshek's Department Store for the first elevator in town when he fell down the shaft.

Mr. McGrath, like Papa, always wore a vest over his shirt, even when digging his garden. He smoked a pipe that he often balanced on a garden fence post. Once the post caught fire, making some excitement.

Another excitement concerned his root beer. We children had been invited to sit around his kitchen table a few times for Mrs. McGrath's homemade bread that he cut with the biggest curved carving knife we'd ever seen. He gave us sips of root beer from slender thin crystal glasses with starbursts etched on the sides. Suddenly a loud popping from the basement caused shouts and laughter as their whole family, glasses in hand, rushed out the door to their outside cellar door facing our yard. We never figured out what all the excitement was about, but Mama must have since she called us home in no uncertain terms.

Awed by all the candles in their darkened parlor, we stared at Mr. McGrath's coffin. Because their front door was up two terraces, the horse-drawn hearse came up our driveway so the coffin could be carried across our yard and down just one flight of steps.

Today old Louis Egelhoff was a sober-faced undertaker in formal tie and tailcoat, though we knew him as a jolly, joke-cracking friend. We tugged at his coattails to ask, "Why do people keep dying?"

"Dying just happens. We have no control over it," said Mr. Egelhoff as he patted our shoulders. Ah, now there was an answer we could accept. Most questions we asked could be answered with a reasonable explanation, just because. We went to see Mama.

Carrie was training Mama to go up steps carefully in her exquisitely simple white evening gown. In front Carrie had cut plain neck and arm holes, but she scooped the back down very low. The gown was form-fitting down to the knees and then a bit flared with three rows of scallops sewn on at ankle-length. It dragged in a slight train at back. "This will look so lovely as you go down the aisle in the processional, and turn to ascend the steps onto the stage. The scallops will drape so prettily as you lift the material at your knee just enough to clear the steps." Mama practiced at the front hall steps until Carrie said fine.

"When can we have Aunt Kay, Mama?" Marjorie asked.

"Why does Aunt Kay keep dying?" Mama sternly replied.

Marjorie stood astride, stomach stuck out, hands behind her back, giving a perfect imitation of Mr. Egelhoff's deep voice. "Dying just happens. We have no control over it."

I spoke up, "We think this Aunt Kay will live for a good long time visiting us."

"Very well. Bring me my purse," Mother smiled.

# The Interview

EVERY OLD HOUSE has endearing qualities with which I'd be content to live. I'm not talking grand old Victorians but ordinary very old housing stock. I love any old house with a porch three steps up to catch the breeze, or even a five-step back stoop, since it provides room underneath for trashcan storage out of neighbor's sight.

Scores of personality houses perch on hills for better views. Some defy gravity, teetering on the edge, approached only by iron-rail-guarded flights of steps; brave houses with hands-on-hips porches defying nature's fiercest elements. Living in them makes a real statement. Then there are careful houses back away from their front terraces in more practical attitude, preparing for anything, my kind of house. They're often clever enough to have a third entrance on the side giving quick access up six steps to kitchen or down six steps to basement. I love all these old houses for their dry useable basements. Don't you love the timid, retiring, shy houses up tight against the bluff walls, hoarding every bit of shelter from storm or sun? They're privacy-loving and often stretch a covering from backdoor to cliff, making a cool summer breezeway or winter snow shield.

Especially lovable are row houses with minimum side yard because they make for neighborliness. You can sit outside your front door and share comments with the entire block, or gossip out the kitchen windows with your neighbor, or share a cook-out. Traffic gives special meaning to houses close to the street, puts you in tune with the seven, three, and eleven o'clock shifts of schools, factories, hospital and nursing homes, service industries. Your city's vital pulse becomes part of you.

Some seemingly plain houses are artfully graced with a little stair window or row of them up a sidewall, or a round window, or a fan light centered under the roof peak. Loveable are those houses with attic windows, or with a drain spout bent under the eaves to go down against the house wall. You can lie in bed listening to rain pattering on the roof or trickling down the spout. Best are the houses without any eaves because absence of overhang allows the first glimpse of moonrise, the fullest view of stars, and broadest sunrise and sunset.

Any house with gingerbread or railings, with shutters or brick chimneys, is precious. Old brick houses with inset keystone arches, or limestone insets over windows deserve to be preserved. All limestone houses are special for the ancient secrets in their very stones. Old frame houses with raised roof or additions at sides or back have an air of ingenuity and hopefulness. All houses with river view are priceless, also two- or more-story houses for the view they command. I love every house with leaning hollyhocks, climbing ivy, or window-box geraniums.

What a wealth of stories each old house contains. Investigating compliance with HUD and city codes revealed a story about preservation worth sharing.

On the new wood porch flooring of a rundown house a lanky senior citizen stretched his feet to gently move his swing. I asked if he was the owner.

"Mrs. Stender owns it," he laughingly replied. "I just live here. I'm Jackson Youngstown." He extended his hand and we shook. Sitting on the porch step, I began thoughtfully filling out forms in my notebook.

**Question:** Do you realize you look like an odd couple?
**Answer:** What kind of a question is that? Moira Stender and Jackson Youngstown; we couldn't be any odder. She's black and I'm white. She's sixty-eight and I'm only fifty. She's a real lady and I'm only an ex-con. Besides, we're not a couple. We're just friends.
**Q:** But you're living in her house. That's odd. Do you pay rent?
**A:** She invited me in, and besides, I work for her. She doesn't have anyone else to do all the work to fix up this old place.
**Q:** Have you even tried to find a real job?
**A:** I tried everywhere. The word got out ahead of me so they all had real pat answers ready about not having any openings. The Rescue Mission took me in right away. I stayed there the seven-day limit, but you have to find a job by then or you're out.
**Q:** Hiring a murderer does have its risks.
**A:** I'm not a murderer! Don't get me riled up! I spent the first

five years in Old Stoney screaming that, but nobody would listen. They'd just slap me back in the hole. Added thirteen years to my sentence for bad behavior, 'til I finally quit protesting. Solitary confinement really beats you down! That metal door slams down and you're trapped. I couldn't take it, so I gave up. I was so quiet they ended up paroling me five years early for good behavior.

**Q:** The courts did convict you as a murderer, didn't they?

**A:** Yes, but my sentence was reduced to manslaughter, with twenty-five years at Anamosa State Penitentiary. I still can't remember what happened. You see, I was high, it was an accident. I was only seventeen and we'd all gone out for the evening on our motorcycles. My whole gang testified against me. My girl was hanging on behind me. They said I popped a wheelie and she fell off. I zoomed around and rode back to see if she was alright, but I ran over her neck. I wheeled around again to look closer and see if she was hurt, but I ran over her head. They said I did it on purpose, but I'd never have hurt her. She was my own cousin, and real pretty. Honestly I can't remember how it happened. My whole family testified against me, and they've never believed me or forgiven me, not a one of them. You see, ever since I was a little kid I liked to do this Arnold Schwarzenegger thing: hunch up my shoulders, flex my arm muscles, and growl to scare anyone who bugged me. I was harmless, but it scared them. Funny, when you have black hair and eyes they call you "dark and handsome," but if you get labeled with murder they say, "Dark and glowering, the eyes of a murderer; we always knew." Believe me, murderers come in all colors. I've lived with them. They kept us in a separate block away from the main body of prisoners. Murderers are dangerous and scary. You never can tell when they'll do something crazy. I learned to keep my back to the wall, and glance right and left at all times. The only thing that saved me from the rest of them was my Arnold Schwarzenegger stance, which would keep them at their distance thinking I might be as dangerous as the rest of them. I tried it on a guard or two, which landed me right back in the hole every time.

**Q:** How did you happen to connect with Moira?

**A:** It was this DREAMS program with the City Housing Department. Moira was so proud to be granted one of these long-term loans with a forgivable mortgage for this derelict of a place, the only one she could afford, but her dream just the same. It's as cheap as paying rent. All she's gotta do is fixer up to safety standards. They're even lending her the tools, the paint, and she's getting the lumber at cost. I saw her on a TV interview while I was staying at the Rescue Mission. They asked her, "Is this really your dream of a home?" and Moira answered, "I told the Housing Department, all it really has to have is a front gate always open so people feel welcome, and a front porch where my friends can sit with me and relax."

Well, I found her address and walked up here to take her up on her offer, and sure enough the gate was open. Actually, it was falling off. I've attached new hinges since, but she still wants it open and welcoming. I was so cold, I curled up on her porch floor with my back against the house, and slept with my head on my satchel. The Rescue Mission gave it to me, along with a hat and change of clothes. You get one suit when you get sprung from the Pen, and a bus ticket. That's how I got here to Dubuque.

No point going back to Wapello where my family and the whole town doesn't want me.

**Q:** What did Moira do when she found you here?

**A:** She scolded me. Moira said, "What are you doing out here in the cold and the fog? Come inside where it's warm. You're welcome to some hot coffee." She never once called me stranger.

**Q:** But does she know she's harboring a murderer?

**A:** Convicted but innocent, I told you! And I told her everything straight off. First she said I could sleep on the couch. Then there was so much to do. Moira'd just retired from a lifetime of work in the kitchen at Mt. Carmel. She said, "You can help me pick up the porch lumber and roof shingles." She drove us down to Spahn and Rose Lumber Yard. I made myself useful by loading up her old van before she'd even thought of all she needed. The porch was first to go. Rotten straight through. I measured and cut these four by fours and rammed them under the roof before it sagged anymore. Then I tore out the old flooring, built a solid frame, and nailed down these new floorboards. The porch is where she likes to sit morning and evening. She likes to watch the view. I like the fresh air. We watch the sunrise and listen to the birds. No birds up at Old Stoney, only some gulls swooping over the yard and screeching around the guard towers.

**Q:** I take it you get along well.

**A:** Moira's been an angel to me. First time we went grocery shopping she handed me the car keys and I was real nervous, but I did alright. She told me to keep them in my pocket. She hands me the small change for something to jingle in my pocket. Thirty years with nothing in your pockets and no personal possessions! She knew it meant a lot. Then she got me a pocket knife, some handkerchiefs, and a billfold of my own. When I'd carried in her groceries, she went right to the sink, poured in a cupful of bleach, and started scrubbing. "No! No! No! No!" I shuddered and leaned my arm against the wall with my head tucked into the bend of my elbow, blubbering like a baby.

"It's the smell of the bleach, isn't it?" She ran the water a good long time to flush it away. "This lemon-scented scouring powder will work just as well." Next she sprayed air freshener around and lit a vanilla candle.

Finally I collapsed onto the couch saying, "I can't bear to smell bleach or naptha, ever again!" Thirty years I'd worked in their laundry. I begged to be assigned somewhere else but we were considered a risk everywhere but there—couldn't be trusted in the license plate manufacturing, might get ahold of a sharp piece of metal. The kitchen was off limits—full of knives. The pharmacy had poisons and drugs. I couldn't even work in the leather shop because of the hammers used to pound the punch for making eyelet holes.

Our job was so monotonous! Steam and heat! Mondays, bedding. Tuesdays, toweling. Wednesdays, uniforms. Thursdays, socks and underwear. Fridays were the worst, with the smell of wet blankets. I would have gladly switched to the cleaning crew, but they said mop and broom handles were potential weapons.

Bleach brings it all back—my eyes and throat sting at the thought. Moira's been an angel! She reads the labels for chlorine-free cleaners and finds different smells to fill the house. She bakes cinnamon rolls a lot, and keeps fresh apples on the table. I'm one lucky guy!

**Q:** And what do you do for her?

**A:** I treat her like the very special lady she is. She likes us to dress up and go to church on Sundays. Luckily, I have my one new suit. I open doors for her. I help her usher at her Rock of Ages Missionary Baptist Church. We're meeting right now at Wartburg Seminary but trying to collect enough money to buy or build a church. I don't know what Moira's told her friends about me. Everyone's been very welcoming and accepting. What's alright for Moira is alright by them. It's not who you are or what your past has been. It's how you act and what you do now that matters to them. I try to please Moira.

**Q:** Are you still sleeping downstairs on the couch?

**A:** Don't you get cute with me! I let drugs steal my life from me at seventeen. Everything passed me by. Never had a chance to grow up, meet people, go places, fall in love. Now I'm too old and it doesn't matter anymore. Actually, I am sleeping upstairs now. Moira had me paint the upstairs rooms. Then we went down to the Mission Store and found me a twin bed and dresser to fit into the smaller room under the eaves. Moira has the nicer furniture in the bigger room. She told me I had to sleep upstairs out of the mess remodeling downstairs. We're tearing off the wallpaper before we patch the ceiling and paint and repaper. Neighbors on the uphill side lent us the stepladder. When it warms up they've promised me the use of a twenty-foot ladder to start laying new roof shingles. I guess they like seeing their neighborhood spruced up.

**Q:** How did you learn to do all this?

**A:** If you can read you can learn to do anything. The Public Library will lend you books on whatever you want. For thirty-

three years I spent my evenings and Sundays at the Pen Library.
I didn't like stories since I felt pretty much down on people. But
I read the Encyclopedia halfway through. Volume A took me
ten years. The next volumes seemed to breeze right along. I was
into the letter M when I was released.

**Q:** Will you finish it?

**A:** If I can find a spare set sometime, I'd like to. Right now I'm
busy.

**Q:** By the way, where's Moira?

**A:** She's upstairs taking a nap. She wants to help me with the
walls but it makes her tired. It makes me feel good. Bit of an age
difference there. She would have invited you in off the porch for
coffee. It's her house. I don't take any liberties here. Just do what
she tells me.

**Q:** Are you happy the way your life has turned out?

**A:** When this whole nightmare started, they locked me up,
threw me a towel, and told me to clean up my own mess. I was
sick when I came down off that high. Had to go through with-
drawal cold turkey. It was agony. My memory was shot. I raged
as the trial progressed. It began to get through to me, the loss of
freedom, and the burden of accusation about something I
couldn't remember or believe. I raged like a madman. It took
years of restraints and confinement before I was myself again,
and then it was too late. I was a prisoner and powerless. Most of
the time I was like a robot. Guess I'm glad I was in with the most
dangerous criminals because I had to stay alert and keep my wits
about me to survive.

**Q:** What have you learned from all this?

**A:** There's the devil to pay when you take drugs. They're a bumpy road to hell, or a detour to a dead end. You say, "Nothing will happen to me." You're right. Nothing happens. Your life is on hold. You quit growing forward. You just spin around in a great big zero. You're cheated out of all your possibilities.

**Q:** But you're happy now?

**A:** I'm happy to have my freedom and to have Moira for a friend. Oddly enough, I have to admit Moira and I are a happy couple.

# Uncle Pud

LOOKING BACK THROUGH all the years to when I was a boy of seven and Uncle Pud hadn't gone off to war yet, that was the only time I was really alive. You could stack up all the calendars of my life and it's like somebody shot a big hole right through them—like I only lived around the edges of the weeks, months, and years. But sometimes if my life felt real and whole during the week, it's like the edges or the weekends had been torn away and scattered to the wind. Nothing has really counted. Robot-like I've shaved my beard and combed my hair thinking the face in the mirror is nobody I'd care to know. Even the cocoa brown walls and the dark chocolate towels give me dark thoughts. My wife, Suzette, says try to think of them as mellow as Nat King Cole's voice, but I'd have preferred lemon yellow.

Today there's a little spark because Cousin Barbie called that she's coming over for a visit. That may be her at the door now.

"Hey, Donnie, hurry down! I've a surprise for you. Looky here!"

"That's a fine painting, Barbie, the best you've ever done."

"It's your Uncle Pud, my Grandfather. Do you recognize him?"

The world stood still while my head whirled around. "That's not Uncle Pud," I whispered. "He was young and strong with curls of gold."

"Well, he's old now and white-haired, but he's still the same Uncle Pud."

"Uncle Pud died in the war. He never came back."

"Now, Donnie, we've told you for years that he came back, but he was just too wounded to come home. You've denied it but it's true."

Out of my gray fog I stared as through a keyhole. There was Uncle Pud's smile, his wide-spaced pale blue eyes, his high cheek-bones, but a halo of white curls around forehead and chin. "Yes, that's what he might look like if he were alive today." My thoughts were pounding at the center of my mind. My lips were numb. An elephant was collapsing my chest.

"Face it, Donnie. You were too little to take it. They didn't tell me, either, for years. But after he'd had enough operations to have visitors, they began to take me once a month. You never would go, not to Iowa City, or Vinton, or DesMoines, or Council Bluffs. You threw shouting fits that Uncle Pud wouldn't stay away unless he was dead, so they quit mentioning him to you. Said you had to be handled with kid gloves. But now he's in *Old Soldiers Home* in Marshalltown and I've painted his picture for you. I want you to know and love him before it's too late. He is your Uncle Pud."

Dark purple curtains behind my eyes shifted. I shuddered. The loss of my Uncle Pud had been more than a little boy like me could bear. I had frozen him away deep in my memory and turned a belligerent face toward the world. My family was cold and preoccupied. They'd never given me attention or love as Pud had. Once I'd lost him, my life slammed shut with a thud. I went through the motions of growing up, school, college, a job like someone else was acting my part. Only when I had a really hot meal, or a really cold shower did I come to for a while and realize I was missing out on something. How I ever got engaged and married and had a little girl of my own was a series of miracle moments for me when my life was hitting on all fours.

"Why don't you come with me on my next visit?"

"You say this is what he looks like now?" Jungle drums pounding between my ears made my words sound a thousand miles away.

"Well, no, this is what he should look like. It's how I see him. Let me remind you his face was mostly blown off on the battle-field. He's only lived by a miracle. It's taken years and years of operations to build him a face with jaws and nose. He's blind, of course, and deaf, but they're teaching him vibrations through a sensor helmet. The doctors all call him their thirty-year war hero."

I grabbed Barbie's hand.

"It'll be alright, she murmured. "You come with me on Saturday. He'll know you. You'll see."

We made the trip to Marshalltown with both excitement and apprehension. My daughter, Suzie, just seven as I had been, wanted to come and I was glad to have her along.

"Remember, now," said Barbie, "Pud is blind and deaf but he'll be glad you're visiting. No hair to speak of, no eyelids, no eyebrows."

I stared at the smooth expressionless face and glass eyes of the older man in a wheel chair. Embarrassed at not knowing him or feeling anything, I went forward and shook his hand. He reached up feeling my arm, so I knelt beside his knee and he felt my face. Then he ran his fingers through my hair, gradually tightening his fingers around my curls, rocking my head gently around in a circle just as he used to do. "It's Uncle Pud! He knows me!" I cried. I hugged his knees as I used to do and a torrent of sobs flooded out, all the years of my seven-year-old self, my lonely teen-age years, my nervous first manhood work years, bursting the dam. He raised my chin to show me as he drew out from his pocket the little tin whistle I'd given him as he went off to war. "He's kept it all these years! He must be smiling inside!"

Uncle Pud gave me the whistle but I folded it back into his fingers. Suzie came to lean against his other knee saying tenderly, "Uncle Pud looks just like Bork." That's her favorite flat-faced TV character from the *Space Ships*. Pud patted her hair, then ran his fingers through both our heads of hair, tightening his hold just enough to rock our heads around in circles.

"Uncle Pud knows you're my daughter, his great-niece," I told Suzie, looking at her in wonder. How had I never noticed? I stared at the golden brown arch of her eyebrows, the sweep of her lashes. Never had I felt such a ruby-red glow of love for her as at this moment.

A white-coated doctor came into the room to stand behind Pud's chair. Laying a respectful but proprietary hand on Pud's shoulder he said, "So Donald here is your Uncle? He's our medical miracle man, a marvel after everything he's gone through. He's taught us so much. For years he breathed and was fed through tubes.

Gradually we've built him jaws and teeth and a nose to breathe through. We've learned by trial and error on him that skin from the upper thigh or just below the shoulder blades makes the best facial skin grafts. Never could do much about lips and lids. The eyes are glass but we're working with him on these sensors to indicate light and shadow and sound vibrations. Learning to eat again took superhuman effort on his part. He learned Braille while at Vinton, and learned to sign in the palm at Council Bluffs. Now he really gives us feedback about the effectiveness of these inventions to simulate sight and sound messages to the brain. The hair is something we really should have worked on more."

"Uncle Pud looks just fine to me," I interrupted, "Truly remarkable." Uncle Pud gave Suzie the tin whistle, then rose and walked confidently to his dresser to lift out and show me his Purple Heart. I hugged him and took off my wristwatch, the only thing I had available, and handed it to him. Pud put it on and then showed me on his other wrist a watch with raised numbers which vibrated when you touched the right hour. He sat down again. "Why the wheelchair?" I asked the doctor.

"Donald can get around well, knows the whole place, but his wheelchair has a chirping motor which warns the other residents so they keep out of his way when he goes down the hall to the dining room. He likes to take his big Braille books down there to read in the sunny bay windows."

Barbie said we'd have to leave since dinnertime was approaching. On the way home I held Suzie's hand. The sky was a Maxfield Parrish masterpiece. "What are you doing?" asked Suzie.

"Whistling," I replied and whistled familiar tunes for her like *Take Me Out To The Ballgame,* and *Hi Ho, Hi Ho, It's Off To Work*

*We Go,* and *Animal Crackers In My Soup.* She laughed when I whistled *The Whistler and His Dog,* starting with a reach for the high note, prancing the melody along, and ending with the dog bark.

At home I rushed to greet my wife, Suzette. With a new-found warmth my forearms wrapped around and pressed her to me, breast to breast. My thumbs traveled up along the bone behind her ears until my fingers sifted through her fragrant silky black hair, tightening to rock her head gently back and forth. Reverently I kissed her forehead, which just came up to my lips. Suzette pulled her head back to say with raised eyebrow, "Well, well, where have you been all my life?"

I reached one arm around Cousin Barbie and hugged them both. "Uncle Pud was great to see. Barbie's painting comes close."

Little Suzie nodded and blew her tin whistle.

# First-Time Volunteers

"WHAT SHALL WE do with the rest of our lives, Lorraine?" giggled Eloise between noisy slurps on her straws. We were carefree, relieved at having just graduated from high school. We twirled on our fountain stools enjoying our Green River sodas.

"I don't know, but jobs shouldn't be hard to find. Not that we have any work experience. Maybe we should volunteer first to find out what we like to do. I don't want to just stay at home and sit around."

"Maybe we can keep files or type reports, or schedules or menus," said Eloise. "Let's try Lady of Lourdes first since it's close, and really big, and must employ lots of workers. But no scrubbing floors, or washing dishes!" We broke into gales of laughter as we planned our strategy.

Next day, dressed in our most grown-up clothes, wearing both hats and gloves, we started up the long brick pathway between grassy slopes toward the huge brick building with its two crenellated tower wings. I nervously rang the bell on the beautiful wooden double doors. We admired the etched glass panels as we waited. A woman in a white uniform greeted us brusquely. "If you're looking for work, you'll have to go to the office. It's upstairs all the way to the back of the long hall." She hurried off. There were old people sitting everywhere we looked. We climbed the stairs in business-like fashion only to be stopped at the top by a well-dressed elderly woman.

"I'm Letitia. What's your name? You're just what I'm looking for. My house is in the tower. Just a minute. I'll be right back. Don't move." All this in a rush, after which she scurried up another flight of stairs to what must have been the tower room.

We stood speechless by the stairs when another lovely lady in a bright red flowing blowsy dress reached out of a doorway and took us warmly by the hands, murmuring, "Come into my parlor. Letitia is higher up, but I have a better view." Her silvery blonde hair swept up in a soft bun. She fingered her long strand of pearls, saying, "I'm Hermione. I've been looking for someone just like you," as she extended her hand.

"I'm Lorraine, and this is Eloise," I answered shaking her hand.

Hermione glanced down. "Your skirt should be a little longer if you work for me." I nodded, making a mental note—hers was about mid-calf. "I don't wear blue. It's so sad. But that will do for you. Personally, I always prefer red. One should try to look cheerful and vibrant, don't you know. Eloise will probably do for Letitia since she's not too particular." Eloise modestly faded into the background while Hermione showed off the view from her expansive windows. "I like to keep an eye on things down at my bank, and on my church, and all the shoppers and cars."

Hermione's room was oblong with institutional yellow walls, but startling to say the least, all bright red and cheerful colors and mostly empty space. All the furnishings were up against the wall opposite the windows, a narrow bed with splashy red spread, an upright piano painted a shocking fuchsia, and a red chair and table with a typewriter. Over the piano hung a wall clock rimmed in, you guessed it, red, and beside it a red, orange, and yellow dartboard with chalkboard center panels. A handful of darts piled atop the piano had rubber tips and there was a box of ground chalk to dip them in so they left marks on the dartboard when thrown.

"Be careful not to slip on the bowling alley," said Hermione pointing out the two long strips of tape stretching down the center of the hardwood floor. She picked up a rubber ball such as we used in grade school to play O'Leary. She rolled it deftly between the strips to clatter against a row of pins lined up against the room's end. "I do think one should keep up one's muscle tone. You can play shuffleboard here, too." She picked up a ruler with a flat board attached across the end and using it as a shuffleboard stick, gave it a swoosh, and put it down again. "I like to keep on the move. Used to ride horses, carriages, bicycles all around town and country." She paused abruptly in her pacing and faced me, "Can you type? You sit down here and type a complaint to those people. I'm too busy or I'd scold them properly myself. Tell them I'm outraged! They've failed me utterly!"

"To whom shall I address this letter?" I asked, fingers poised above the keys to show my typing expertise.

"The newspapers, the magazines, any one of them. They're all impossible. They never express my opinions. None of them reflect our mainstream society anymore. One can't find a truly satisfying news report these days. Their words are stuff and nonsense."

While I proceeded to type a vague but reproachful letter "to whom it might concern," Hermione nodded agreement over my shoulders. A little nondescript man in gray sidled into the room. Hermione pulled the pink piano stool up to the end of the table, commanding, "Neville, get out your checkbook. This is Lorraine. She'll be coming in every day bright and early." She raised an eyebrow at me. "Say about ten. Would ten to two suit you? That way we can go downstairs and dine at the club together." She and Neville began negotiating about my wages and she finally handed me a check. "Sundays off, of course," she smiled as she led me to the door. As Eloise and I made a quick exit, we heard someone say, "Neville! Come out of there and stay out of the ladies' rooms!"

Eloise decided not to go up to Letitia's tower room that day. We hurriedly left the premises. Upon attaining the street, we examined the check. "Let's go straight to the bank and cash your check," said Eloise. "That's pretty good pay for one short letter."

"Ah, so you've been to Mrs. Tannerdyce, I see," said the teller thoughtfully handling the check. "You know these are long-expired checks written on a long-extinct bank. Neville was once an accountant. We handle Mrs. Tannerdyce's trust account here but, unless a doctor writes an order that she needs a paid attendant, we can't pay you anything. You were just a volunteer companion today. You no doubt made a ga-ga old lady very happy. She was once a real power in many official organizations. Nowadays she's gone into a fantasy. I paid her a courtesy call last month and she still looks pretty good for her age."

"Listen, Eloise," I said once we were outdoors, "if that's volunteer work, it's not too bad. It's surely different and it might be a blast. Why don't you visit Letitia tomorrow? We'll try to check in properly at the office first to make sure somebody knows what we're doing and it's on the record."

"Sure, Lorraine, why not? I'm all for new experiences. Who knows? If we can be useful maybe it will lead to paid work someday. Can't wait to see Letitia's fantasyland. But you have to come with me the first time I go up in the tower, agreed?"

Eloise and I shook on it and went off to the soda fountain to celebrate our venture into the real world as volunteers.

Early next morning Eloise and I, dressed in green plaid skirts and sparkling white midi blouses, hurriedly gulped our grape sodas while plotting our day.

"We need to be at Lady of Lourdes office by 9:30 to ask for jobs and explain our volunteer efforts with Hermione yesterday. Remember, Lorraine, she's expecting you at ten a.m.," said Eloise.

"And I promised to go with you up to Letitia's tower room," I replied.

We never made it to the office for Letitia rushed down two flights of stairs in a whirlwind, demanding, "Where were you? I waited for you!" She spouted, "Never mind. There's work to be done."

She grabbed each of us by the hand, guiding us upstairs with little pulls and pushes.

Hermione peeked out of her door too late, as Letitia triumphantly shoved us into her tower room and slammed her door. "There, now aren't you glad you came to my house?" she panted, leaning against the door to recover. "Just take a look at that far-away river from my windows, and see down there, you can see bird nests in those trees."

Letitia wore a nondescript long gray gown over which she'd tied a deep-pocketed kitchen apron. Her gray hair was wound up into a bun from which protruded two long knitting needles. Though her demeanor was stern, lurking smiles kept surfacing to the corners of her mouth. Her room was a-clutter with old furniture and piles of junk. One corner of this small square room expanded into a two and a half yard wide circle—the tower—with room enough for a rocking chair and table there in the sunlight pouring through two dusty curved glass windows.

"Heavens to Betsy! I've been meaning to wash those. Nobody does a lick around here! Goodness gracious but I used to keep a clean house!" She determinedly squelched her smile into a frown. "And these stairs will be the death of me yet! You can't imagine how hard they are on my old crippled joints. I can barely get around from the pain!" Letitia agilely scurried about searching under pile after pile of junk.

"Are you looking for something?" Eloise asked politely.

"My knitting needles. Someone's walked off with them!"

"My name's Lorraine," I interrupted. "I think these are what you want." I gently pulled the lost needles from her bun, which promptly fell into straggles behind her. "I'm glad to have met you, but must be going down to Hermione's. Elaine will visit with you awhile."

"Nonsense! Just make yourselves useful straigtening out my colors."

Letitia swooped up from her bed piles of half-wound balls and skeins of yarn, shoving them at us. She picked up her half-knitted afghan all brightly colored in a zig zag design. Plopping into her rocker, she searched for the place to recommence her knitting. Dutifully we sat on either end of the bed with the yarn between us.

"Let's unsnarl this flame-orange one first," said Eloise.

We each unsnarled ends and began to wind balls. Was that a snore? We looked up to see Letitia fast asleep. Silently we wound for a bit.

Into the room swished a busy nurse in white uniform. "Letitia?" she questioned, bending to look closely. Next she began emptying from Letitia's deep apron pockets bright knick knacks, vases, figurines, a silver comb, a toy poodle, artificial flowers. With one foot she hooked a footstool, lifted Letitia's shoes with one hand, slid the footstool under, and straightened her now-elevated legs. Nurse put a comforter over Letitia saying, "She'll sleep for a good two hours. Wears herself out running around. Why are you here?"

"We're Lorraine and Elaine. Letitia brought us up here before we could find the office to apply for work."

"I don't know about jobs, but you can help me return these on your way."

We looked mystified and Nurse explained, "It's a compulsion or something. She knows it's stealing because she only takes things when nobody's looking. Maybe a wood carving of the *Praying Hands* by Dore and a wooden-framed embroidery motto, *God Bless This Home*. She hung them in their proper places on the wall outside Letitia's room. We proceeded down the hallway carrying the objects which Nurse now returned to their various owners, some of whom were annoyed, others patiently understanding and glad of their safe return.

Entering the office, I explained, "I'm Lorraine and this is Elaine. We've visited Hermione and Letitia the past two days but are really seeking employment."

"What we need here are volunteers with a knack for helping older people," said the person in charge. "If you prove useful it might lead to something. Could you come every afternoon from two to four during game time to help residents, and keep them from quarreling or falling asleep during games? Or several days a week? At least call if you're not coming?" The matron raised a hopeful eyebrow.

"We'd love to come," said Eloise.

"We'll be the grownups for a change," I added.

# Bird Sitting isn't for Babies

CITY SMOKE AND dust-covered windows dinged the sunlight and obscured the skyline. Time to clean windows before the fall chill made having them open unpleasant. Sis and I began washing them with vinegar and water and polishing them dry with newspapers. What a view! Mrs. Rath, now living alone on the corner of Heeb and Seminary Hill, had her upstairs converted to an apartment to rent to young women. Three windows in a row added light and looked up to Madison Park and down across town to the Mississippi.

"What's that white bird in the park trees? A gull?" In a flash it sailed toward our open windows and into the room.

"Look out!" cried Ermine, covering her head. She needn't have bothered—the bird flew to the highest perch in the room, the wooden drapery pole.

"No, that's not a gull. See its crest and fat yellow beak, and its tail is too long. Maybe a parrot."

"Well, scoot it out of here, Evelyn. It scares me."

"Now, Ermine, if we just stay very quiet and don't frighten it, perhaps it will fly outside of its own accord." As if on cue, this big white bird fluttered its wings, walked across the pole to the draperies and started to clamber down them, its big sharp claws clutching the material firmly. Reaching out a claw, it turned upright and grabbed the embroidered round shade pull to hang and swing a bit, then reached out the other claw and fluttered to the draperies on the far side. It clawed sedately up the curtains and roosted once more atop the wooden pole. We stared open-mouthed.

"I think it's a trained bird, a pet. Not a parrot but a cockatoo." We studied the bird. His strong beak hooked downward. His beady black eyes were rimmed in pink, and the merest suggestion of pale pink tinged his jaw feathers. Otherwise he was cloud-white and about twelve inches long.

"What was he doing in the park? Perhaps he was lost or escaped his home," said Ermine.

"Do you suppose it's hungry?" I asked. "Polly want a cracker?" Our bird immediately swooped down to the table and began turning over edges of magazines first with beak, then with one claw, to look under them. We hurried into the kitchen to round up food and water.

"Remember when Evangeline babysat the Zellenz family's precious fifty- year-old parrot? What did she feed him?" asked Ermine. That was back when we were in college. For a whole week our older sister, Evangeline, had cared for the Zellenz's parrot while they attended a family wedding in Chicago. Evangeline had earned five dollars, a huge sum in those days. Their parrot was a rare and beautiful parrot with blue and green wings and tail and a red chest and back. It had a cross-bar stand with feeding cups at each end for water, seeds, fruit, and meat. Evangeline kept it fed with sunflower, pumpkin, and squash seeds, a stick of celery, and wedges of apple or orange every day, and a strip of bacon or tiny ball of hamburger. It was a jungle carnivore which normally would feed on small birds or rodents, snakes or frogs, plus fruits, vegetables, and seeds in the wild. Its beak was dangerous, made for tearing things apart. She'd been warned not to hand feed it. There was a long slender brass chain attaching one leg to the stand. At the Zellenz's house it had freedom to fly around in their sun porch, while at our house it stayed on its perch or walked around on the dining room table Evangeline kept covered with newspapers to catch its droppings. Nevertheless, it managed to splatter and scatter seeds as far as the mantelpiece and buffet, which necessitated a real clean-up job when he left. That parrot displayed no tricks, just a jungle-shattering shriek at daybreak, and unpleasant squawks during the entire time mother's piano students took their lessons, and we had to keep the dining room door shut against his din. That was probably a good idea anyway, since tropical birds are susceptible to drafts. Every night Evangeline would slip his sheltering night cover over the stand so he could sleep in comfort.

"We have no seeds," I said. "Let's make a few cracker sandwiches with peanut butter or cheese spread in between and see which he prefers." We placed measuring cups on the table with water, apple, and crackers. Our bird seized a peanut butter cracker sandwich in one claw and pecked at it viciously, crumbs and bits spewing in all directions. Then he proceeded to daintily peck up each and every last bit. His tongue was black and very agile, but drinking was a splattery shower.

We watched our bird, who was now ignoring us. I ventured, "Is your name Polly? Molly? Bobbie? Lonnie? Ronnie?"

Attention caught, he immediately called out, "Ronnie! Ronnie! Pretty boy! Toy boy! Atta boy! Lover boy! Ronnie!"

"Your name is Ronnie?"

Once again came this unexpected spiel, "Atta boy, Ronnie, pretty boy, toy boy, lover boy, Ronnie!" He flew to my shoulder, clutching me firmly, much to my trepidation, until he leaned his head against my cheek, and seemed to stroke it with his own.

"Now that shows he loves someone and they have loved him," said Ermine. Regretfully she added, "Oh, Evelyn, we'll have to advertise for lost parrot owners."

"Better, yet, we can call young Dr. Vanderloo to ask if he knows anyone who's missing a pet cockatoo. Or the pet store owner down on Central Avenue. Someone is surely sick with worry over him." Alas, the pet store owner knew a man in Platteville who'd bought a cockatoo last year. We called the number he gave us and received a joyous clamoring at the other end of the line about our news. He'd come first thing in the morning to pick up his pet.

"Where will Ronnie roost for the night?" We rummaged through the apartment, finally dragging from the back of the closet an old hula hoop. We hung it firmly from the floor lamp stand. "No. Too low. It's drafty down there." We next stood the lamp stand upon the table with the hula hoop hanging. Ronnie must have liked the height because he perched at the bottom of the hoop as it swung gently.

"How would you like a pillow case for a night cover?" I asked. Ermine and I ripped a pillowcase open and fastened it carefully around Ronnie's improvised stand. Not a peep. Figuring he must be tired, we tiptoed from the room.

Before we had time to wash and comb next morning, our Platteville man rang the bell and dashed up the stairs. We showed him where Ronnie was. He lifted the pillowcase hesitantly asking, "Ronnie?" There was no doubt in our minds this was Ronnie's owner. They were billing and cooing. Ronnie perched on his owner's shoulder, snuggled against his collar, stroked his beard, pecked him with little kisses. It would have been pathetic to hear a grown man uttering babytalk, except that the same feelings resonated in our hearts.

After their reunion the man asked how we'd found his pet and surmised that Ronnie might have been answering Nature's call to search for a mate when he'd flown off. "Couldn't find his way home, I guess. I prayed he'd have sense enough to come in out of the cold." He took from his wallet twenty-five dollars, insisting we take it for the care and consideration we'd shown in returning his pet. They proceeded down the steps, Ronnie never so much as shifting from his shoulder perch even as they got into his car and drove away.

The going rate for babysitting birds had gone up over the years, as had the value of the dollar. We suddenly remembered the rejoicing the Zellenz family felt at finding their beloved pet safe and healthy. Had Evangeline cried as they took their pet away? We couldn't remember, but we certainly did at Ronnie's departure. We'd known him for less than a day, but what a price to pay for this glimpse into the love shared between a pet and its owner. Painful, but priceless.

# Down-Home Christmas

SINCE WE LIVED halfway up North Main Hill, Christmas in my early childhood meant going down to Grandma Herrmann's on 25th and Central Avenue where Papa grew up. Christmas actually began Christmas Eve with us going uphill to Grandma Campbell and Aunt Grace's apartment tucked under the eaves of the brick house owned by Papa across from Madison Park on North Main.

My mother was a fine pianist and her sister, Grace, was a gifted violinist, so Aunt Grace's Christmas tradition was hot chocolate and carols. As she and Mama played we all sang, with Cousin Robert, too. Then she'd give each of us a little Bunte's chocolate cream Santa Claus and a Betty Jane's chocolate-dipped orange rind stick to enjoy. Her instructions were, "Hurry home and get to sleep in time for Santa to fill your stockings."

What awakened us on Christmas morn was sometimes the magical hush of new-fallen snow, but always the clatter and sharp ring of the horse's hooves drawing the milk wagon up the brick street. If the frozen cream rose up out of the bottle neck, Mama would slice it onto our cereal. In our stockings we found a rare and treasured orange, an apple, and some peanuts in the shell, some hard candy, and a few little wooden toys.

We opened our gifts and again hurried up North Main and down Seminary Hill to church at St. Luke's. Then it was back uphill to our house and finally down home to the excitement of Christmas at Grandma Herrmann's. With Papa's four children and Uncle Oscar's eight, plus his three foster children from Hillcrest Baby Fold, and all the aunts and uncles, the house grew joyfully boisterous. Our grandparents always felt Christmas was for children.

Grandpa Richard Herrmann would have the front parlor sliding doors mysteriously shut while we gathered and deposited our wraps in the back hall. Grandma's domain was the middle parlor where she'd stretched out her dining table with its infinite number of extension boards, and the back dining room and breakfast room with their tables, and her kitchen. She and Aunt Rosalie had prepared chicken dinner with enough for all. Settees were drawn up from the walls to the table, and all the dining chairs in the house were used. She seated four or five of us little ones on each settee. I recall the horsehair sofa itched unbearably, but Grandma Hermann, who was mostly smiles, would say sternly, "Don't wiggle!"

Grandma always used her fragile Haviland china with the green thistle pattern for these occasions, plus the lovely pale pink kitchen china. I loved the tiny salt dishes and curved flute-edged bone dishes. Grandma always served a tureen full of gefilte fish, a whitefish in a cool jelled slightly tart sauce full of sliced carrots, cloves, peppercorns, and bay leaf. Aunt Rosalie's specialty was candied crab apples. All the aunts brought their special koffee kucken, some topped with rows of slices apples or pears, some with lemon and sesame seeds, some with candied citron or other fruits. Aunt Bertha's was best smothered in cinnamon sugar. Grandma Lina Jungk Herrmann and her sisters, Clara, Selma, Edna, Emma, and sister-in-law Anna, would line their cakes up on the sideboard, slice thin wedges off each to sample, then generously say to each other, "Yours got good," and anxiously, "Did mine get good?" We devoured the lot while the women cleared tables and went to "warsh and wrench the dishes in the zink."

Now was time for Grandpa Richard Herrman to preside. Uncle Arthur would open the sliding doors to the front parlor. There to our "Ohs," and "Ahs," Grandpa with a taper would light finger-sized red candles all over the Christmas tree. We gazed in rapt admiration at the twinkling candlelight cast on the gleaming ornaments and big top star. His tree was always sparse to avoid fire. He and Uncle Arthur soon extinguished the candles and turned on overhead lights.

Grandpa's treeholder was a red-outfitted troll-like Santa, with long white beard just like Grandpa's, standing on a yard-square platform surrounded by little white fencing. A peculiar mixture of Old and New Testaments, the fence penned in a regular Noah's Ark of sets of animals, farm animals, German furred animals.

We each received from Grandpa a silver dollar and one very special gift, usually something educational. For the older boys it was a working steam engine, or a camera, a radio set, or a gyroscope, Egyptian magic tricks, or the like. My sister, Grace, one year received a Schoenhut miniature grand piano with stool upon which she could sit and play the two and a half octaves of keys. My favorite gift was a little working washing machine with real rubber rollers to wring out the water. The machine had a hand crank to make the metal dolly suds the doll clothes well. Marjorie and Adele one year received porcelain-faced dolls with real hair curls and moveable elbow and knee joints. Baby brother Richard got a collapsible rocking horse chair one year and a furry horse on wheels to ride like a kiddie car the next.

This was Grandpa's informal time. He'd lead us littler ones in a circle singing "Ring Around Aunt Rosalie," and Uncle Arthur would give us horsey rides on his big black boot. By then we were anxious for the museum tour. Grandpa always patiently led the way explaining, answering questions to make sure we understood all about what was in his hall cabinets full of rocks, fossils, stalactites, stalagmites, minerals, shells, eggs, plants, birds, fish, money, and mysterious specimens. Finally we'd get upstairs to rooms full of Indian artifacts. A rod on a red stand suspended the skeleton of Chief Peosta. (Grandpa thought he was giving the Chief a place of honor, but one year Fulton School children thought it disrespectful, so Chief Peosta was eventually given a formal burial out at his original resting place at the Mines of Spain near Julien Dubuque's castle monument.)

To me the most thrilling moment was when Grandpa opened his little round pill box to show us, through a long-handled looking glass, the ear drums (anvil, stapes, and stirrup) which Uncle Arthur had sifted from the skull of Chief Peosta, when his skeleton was first dug up and laid out in the parlor downstairs. Cousin John took very clear pictures through the magnifying glass.

As we came down from the cold rooms I often thought what a patient woman Grandma was to not complain when Grandpa filled four rooms of their house to overflowing with museum pieces, from skulls and bones and rattlesnake skins to stuffed fish and other animals, real Indian clothing and weapons, rifles, swords, canoes, and so many other things.

We gathered round the big square grand piano in the parlor for carols. Grandpa had a violin always out on the piano ready to play. His sons also played violins, and most of the grandchildren. Then Cousin Selma took over at the fancy carved pump organ. She'd pull *Gilbert and Sullivan Operettas* from among piles of music and have us all singing parts. John, William, and David already had fine male voices, but Paul, Jimmy, and Richie had to sing with us girls. We liked the *"Three Little Girls from School Are We"* bits and the boys went to town on *"We'll Polish Up the Handles On the Big Brass Doors."* Whenever we didn't help enough with pumping the foot pedals, the music would fail, and Selma would make us all hold that note until we got the organ pumped enough to go on with the music. Thus we ended up in gales of laughter.

Grandma Herrmann would end the festivities by serving coffee to grownups, and milk and sugar tea to us children in her fragile Japanese cups and saucers so richly painted you could feel the gold beading against your lips as you drank. Thoroughly satisfied, we trudged home along Central Avenue, then over Francis Street, stopping at the corner of Kaufmann and Heeb to listen to the restless stirring and clomping of draft horse hooves inside the huge limestone barn of the Meadowgold Dairy. We climbed North Main in twilight seeing in most windows we passed the twinkling lights of Christmas trees.

# Perry Peregrine

MISSISSIPPI SILVERS BLUE beneath the pale moonlight. As
the moon goes down, I open a sleepy eye to the pre-dawn temperature change and listen for the train wheezing up the valley. I
love to watch the river change to lavender-hued ribbons trailing
around floating black islands as mauve pink creeps up the skyline. My mate and I stir our feathers, flex our hunched shoulders,
lift one leg, then the other on our rocky perch beside our sleeping
brood of three chicks tucked into a deep hole in the rocky quarry
facing the dawn.

My mate is beautiful, mine for life. She's a bit bigger than I
with a tawny front speckled with brown dots progressing into
thin brown stripes all the way down to her tail. She's a devoted
mother and will perch here for six weeks guarding our young.
Her eyes are beautiful bright brown slightly rimmed in white.
She can look straight at me, the thing which makes us peregrines
such great hunters: keen eyesight and full frontal vision. That
and the fact that we have a brow ridge almost as deep as the
eagle's to shield our eyes from the sun's glare. She retained her
brown hood, wings and back and the brown streak down the

cheeks, which distinguishes us peregrines from other falcons. (It's somewhat wider than a cheetah's facial tear streak.) Since maturing, my brown has turned to slate blue-black from hood to tail with pronounced dark cheek streak, though my chest remains like hers. There is faintly darker barring on our wings and tail feathers. Our beaks are dark, hooked and powerful, and our legs are dark yellow with hooked strong claws.

When I was courting her, I fed her copious amounts to prove I could be a good food provider. With much bobbing up and down, with chittering calls and with breathtaking aerial revolutions I stood out from the rest of the falcon colony along the rock face.

My mate laid a round egg in this little cave in the rocks. I must admit we're not much into nest building. After she laid the second egg she started to incubate them for about twenty-eight days. She laid a third egg, as one is liable to roll off the ledge.

Word has it that we peregrines alerted humans to the danger of organochlorine insecticides by our sudden decline back in 1950s to the point of extinction in the Northeast. But environmental laws have made our reintroduction and regrowth as a species possible.

Squeaking in the shell indicated our chicks might be starting to cut their way out with their egg teeth. Actually, this high spot along the beak is later useful to crush the necks of our prey. Newly hatched, our young ones were a laughable sight. With bleary, partly opened eyes, with heavy heads, their feeble necks were unable to hold up their huge beaks for more than a moment. They were thinly covered in off-white prepennae down. Their mother brooded them only two days but has never ceased perching at the opening so they can't fall from our nest site. In seven days the second down or preplumulae enveloped them in a comically voluminous white fluffy coating (like so much popcorn), soon to become their under feathers as real feathers sprout out. Their bills and taloned feet are growing strong so they can feed themselves on food dropped into the nest. They've become more active, shuffling about the nest, starting to stand, as true feathers grow.

This has been my most trying time, but I'm a born hunter, up to the challenge. I have five mouths to feed: my mate, myself, and my three chicks who require as much as an adult. I'd better get moving.

Thick mist will soon be billowing up off the Mississippi into white clouds. In the chill damp I know I must grab a quick bite to stoke my energy for the day's effort. An incoming bat, any rodent before he goes underground, a weevil, ground squirrel, or a frog will do, but I have to capture five quickly for my family's first feedings. Then I'm off to my true calling.

It will be weeks before their mother will begin to trade off the watch with me so she can go out and help with the hunting. Our chicks have already lost weight while growing rapidly, but this may assist in their first efforts at flight.

My mate taught the chicks to back up to the edge of our cave and defecate over the side so she can keep the nest site clean. Eventually she'll leave them alone (at about 120 days) while we hunt, and you can bet they'll try their wings while we're out of sight. Right now they'll see me off to work.

Perched, I sight my prey, tighten my plumage, bob my head up and down to get a good perspective. Court house pigeons are my favorite prey, or those smart-alecky crows or noisy jays, thrushes, bats, gulls, even ptarmigan, quails, pheasants, or owls. If it's flying, I wait until it's out of sight or behind an obstacle before starting my pursuit. Now until sunrise is the safest flying time for me when I can use small rising thermals to soar above the cliffs for flight advantage. After nine, larger thermals rise and can lift eagles or turkey vultures, whom I prefer to avoid. From 200 meters up I can pick up a pigeon playing on a ledge or a dove on a wire. However, I soar from 500-1500 meters to stoop (dive) at birds in flight. When my mate is available we make a beautiful team over water. Seeing a bird crossing the river at 2.5 kilometers away, I can strike in mid-air. As it falls, she, coming from 100 meters behind me, swoops under and catches it before it drops to the water. Without her, I stay over land.

Only about one attack in ten is successful, so I work busily. Fresh prey is delivered immediately to the nest, but every fifth one I bite off the head and eat it rapidly, perching to pull out the feathers and eat the rest of the body, bones and all.

I'm a Peregrine. When seizing, I approach from behind level with my prey, then fling my pelvis, legs, and feet forward and upward to grip. When soaring on high, I stoop or dive faster than a bullet, passing over almost level, with legs flexed, and I strike downward with all four toes extended, closing them instantly around the quarry. I try to give a glancing soccer kick rather than a football drop kick, or I might break my own strong legs. Sometimes when prey is heavier or bigger, I have to strike repeatedly at head or neck. The central skill is the kick.

My speed is for the approach. I check in flight, not necessarily to attack, but to assess my chances. Eagles often stoop at a passing gull just to terrify it playfully, so please excuse me if I can't resist taking a mock swipe at a passing pigeon just to scare the daylights out of him.

My very long middle toe is for aerial killing, in contrast to the eagle's powerful hind toe and long talon which lets him kill and grasp fish or rabbit, crashing down on them with the forceful grip of his front talons while the back talon pierces a vital spot. My *fleor digitorium longus* and *flexor hallucis longus* contract to hold and strike, and my *tibialis anterior* muscle flexes the knee joint as I hold my prey close to my body.

First there is the headlong rush as I stoop with split-second timing and accuracy, then the smack of impact as I strike my prey dead in the air and seize it in my foot, then the leisurely descent to carry it home, the victorious meal-winner of the family.

We Peregrine Falcons never need fly slowly. Consider our design. Inside our nostrils a round tubercle acts as an air baffle at high speed. Our blunt bullet-shaped bodies can dive at 80 meters per second accelerating, to 125 meters at terminal velocity. Our medium-long thin tail steers and maneuvers while our wings lift and propel with overlapping functions. We can steer in confined spaces, or brake while soaring and our tails spread to increase lift. Both can be raised or lowered to slip air, accelerating or slowing descent. Our strong shoulders cant our wings this way or that for balance.

You can recognize me in flight because my longer more pointed wings are different than the hawk's rounded and blunt wings. My long pointed primary feathers are barely emarginated for speed in dive. Emargination produces wing slots to reduce turbulence at wingtip, which is useful in landing, and in preventing stalling in flight. I can widely separate my spread feathers so each can act as an individual aerofoil or flying surface, as if I had a solid wing with a whole series of little wings attached to the tip. These bend individually under load, fractionally one above the other, something like a biplane or triplane, increasing the lift at the wing extremities. It helps large birds like me gain soaring lift but still avoid extremely long wings like an albatross which can't land easily on the ground or in branches as I can. The folded wings of an albatross look like a joke, the folded long ulna gives the vulture his hunched shoulders, gives the eagle a regal appearance, while my shoulders seem just right, a happy medium.

I'm 16 inches long with a 40-inch wingspan, while the eagle is 32 inches with an 80-inch wingspread, exactly twice my size. Our wing load depends on the volume of our length or the weight carried by any given unit area of our wings.

The lower the wing load the slower the bird can fly and still remain airborne. High wing load gives high diving speed. Wing load controls the length of the turning radius. The lower the load, the smaller the circle. I can turn tight circles; the heavier the bird relative to its frontal area, the higher the terminal velocity it reaches before wing resistance prevents further acceleration. High wing load improves gliding angle at high speeds and aids cross-country soaring. Adding ballast reduces rate of sink at high speeds, but I soar high, circle tightly, and dive fast.

So you see, I'm perfect—not too heavy, not too light. I can out-dive them all, if not out-fly them all. Only the Prairie Falcon is faster than I. I know my place. I'm Perry Peregrine and Perfect is my middle name. Busy morning sounds gear up as I soar high over a 100-mile range, spotting easy targets first but saving the

lengthier hunts for later in the day. Plucking up pigeons decorating the Court House steps means ready lunch for my family, since
those pinheads never learn. Hiding was left out of their vocabu-
lary. I can readily attack a lone crow, but when three or more
flock to harry me with their cawing, I settle quietly among the
tree branches where they soon lose sight of me and forget where
I am. Then I resume my hunt.

While the eagles are still nesting in the tallest trees of Eagle
Point Park and vultures are roosting on the water tower, I'm king
of the skies and brother to the streaming winds. Eagles prefer fish,
vultures prefer to clean up the road kill, and the gullible gulls will
dine on anything anywhere from garbage dumps to parking lots,
but I am a born sportsman. I'll chase a bird in flight, giving him a
sporting chance, rather than target a sitting duck any day. I hunt
down only what I need to keep my family happily fed.

Peregrines are at home worldwide. Old World custom used us
for hunting and fetching like a dog. We would rather be free and
slave to no one, flying for the exhilaration of tilting and turning,
plummeting and soaring, lifted by the wind to glide with sunlight
glinting across our wings, at home in the sky.

# Mama and Vladimir Horowitz

WE COUCH POTATOES shot up to crowd around the TV screen, peering at Horowitz's splayed out hands playing the piano keys with the flats of his fingers. He'd come down off his fingertips to the balls of the fingers just like Mama had done. Had he had her heart attack?

We remembered his televised 1967 concert, his hands in the arched and curled chicken coop position, freeing the thumbs to dart back and forth under the fingers with the greatest rapidity up and down the keyboard—the same Leschetizky Method which Mama used and taught.

Now after a mysterious twelve-year absence he made a televised appearance at the Met. The exquisitely controlled tone and feeling of the master pianist was always in his fingertips, but now he was achieving the same perfection while playing on the balls of his fingers. Had the sensitivity of his peripheral nerves died back so now he had to find a new way of producing the tones he wanted? That's what happened to Mama.

Ada Betsy Campbell was the darling of Dubuque's pianistic world, Professor Kleine's star pupil and teacher. Professor Kleine's Dubuque Academy of Music was situated on the second floor at the corner of Eleventh and Main. Lina Kleine had been a pupil of Clara Schuman and gave quality to the Academy. While the Academy had fine teachers, Mama was most in demand as a soloist. She appeared with the Minneapolis Symphony, but then she pretty much retired to marry Henry Herrmann and raise four children, though she continued to perform and give piano lessons from our home.

I remember the concerts given by the Academy. After detaching the legs of the big Baldwin and Schwinn grand pianos, they'd turn them on their sides to lower them out the upper story windows with block and tackle. They were taken up Eleventh Street to the First Congregational Church for graduation recitals or up Main Street to St. Luke's for concerts.

Most memorable were times they built a platform upon which to assemble four grands. Such a symphony of sound as eight pianists, two at each piano, brought classics to resounding life! Mrs. Kleine and Mama played at one. Then there were Marjorie Wilson (organist at First Congregational Church) and Martha Kintzinger (organist at St. Luke's) at the second. Playing the third were Georgia Nix who lived in the Fourteenth Street Faneuil Hall Apartments and Vivien Lee who was related to the Ryans, great friends of General Grant's. She drove the last Duesenberg in Dubuque.

The other pianists were Clara Hetherington from up on West Thirteenth and Edith Groff, the last living Academy teacher, who ended up teaching at University of Dubuque.

To grow up in the home of a pianist is a treasure beyond belief. Every morning Mama would rise early, put breakfast on the table, call us, and then go into the parlor to play her piano while we dressed and ate. Off we trudged to school, wrapped in her lovely melodies.

"Why is Mama playing in the dark?" I asked one day.

"Leave her alone," said Papa. "She's listening hard."

The day before, Mama had come home weeping bitterly, "I didn't play well." Janet and Dr. Fritz, her friends, had her perform at their son's wedding at dusk on the patio amid glowing hurricane lamps. "The keys were slippery with moths attracted to the light, but I fear it was my fingers. I'll take a year off and play for no one until I get back my technique," she ruefully declared.

Despondency dimmed our house. No parlor light, no melody, only endless scales, arpeggios, exercises up and down the keyboard. We'd tiptoe past the dark doorway to not disturb her efforts. It was a long dismal year before she turned on her piano lamp. Peeking in from the hall, I whispered, "Mama, you've come down off your fingertips!"

"I've found a new technique I can live with," she smiled and played my favorite Chopin Nocturne. Once again she was satisfied with pianistic perfection. Unfortunately Mama died that summer, halfway between the weddings of her two oldest daughters. Her heart valves had been damaged by a year-long bout of rheumatic fever years ago and had crumbled, causing blood clots. That was 1944 and decades before doctors discovered they could identify silent heart attacks by the dying back of nerves in the fingertips, long before antibiotics and blood thinners. Mama only knew her artist's touch was changed.

Mama had to go it alone, and so did Vladimir Horowitz.

# Meet Your Neighbor

SHE IS A lovely lady alone in any neighborhood like yours. Her house is little and old, and so is she. She is in her eighties, wears glasses, dresses carefully with matching hat and handbag, often wearing gloves or a tasteful bit of jewelry. She rides the bus to the doctor's office, grocery store, and shopping mall. She attends church frequently, but must rely on friends' rides for Sunday Service. She enjoys daytime clubs, and her volunteer hours helping others add up each week. She keeps busy.

In spring and fall, someone comes for a two- or three-day visit. "This is my son," she says with pride. (Or son-in-law. Or nephew.) "He's changed the screens and storm windows for me." (Or trimmed the grass or hedge. Or put in an overhead front door light.) All her children have made their homes in other states while she stays on in the old family home.

"Am I lonely? Not a bit," she lies. But she'll never consider leaving her home. She maintains family tradition and a home place for her children. Her daughters phone or write often. They visit or take her on trips but know she's comfortable in her independence. When they leave it's always with a choice piece of heritage: a photo album, the family Bible, a footstool, or a hand-made afghan. She tries to hand out her belongings to whoever will take them. "Makes less for me to dust."

"Come for tea," she says. She carefully lifts down her blue and white willow pattern teapot from the shelf. When alone, it's instant tea in white crockery cups edged in the orange and black lines of Roshek's. She shows them to me. "I got these at auction when their store closed down. They're wonderful handwarmers," she adds cupping one in both hands. But for company she loves to smell orange pekoe tea brewing in the willow pot.

Next she's likely to lay out daintily hand-painted china cups and saucers. "These were my mother's and the plates came from Great Aunt Lillian and Mazie." She shows all her china treasures lined up on wall shelves where she can see them. Each has a story and a happy memory she relives in the telling.

"Have a Girl Scout cookie," she offers. "I don't bake any-more, and these seem to last forever. My appetite for sweets has shrunk."

"Do you still have friends in the neighborhood?" we might ask. "Do you like living here alone? Have you thought about going to a retirement home where there's always someone to talk to?"

"I must like this neighborhood since I've lived here eighty years. I get along fine. I play cards at the neighbor's across the street every Tuesday. There are young people who'll cut my grass or shovel my snow cheaply. Sometimes they do it for free." She shows off her cupboard shelves full of single serving cans which make the weight of grocery bags less. She shows you her sewing machine where she does her crafts or busy work. She strokes her hands lovingly over the living room piano she used to play before arthritis forced her to stop.

One lady's daughter is a travel agent who has taken her along to Paris several times with her tours. They always visit the tomb of Chopin to lay a red rose in remembrance and a thank-you for beautiful music. Many do this and acquaintances are struck up. In the conversation she always tells proudly about being from mid-America and extolling the beauty and attractions of living along the Mississippi.

Another lady has been to the Japanese Tea Garden in Golden Gate Park in San Francisco where a New Yorker struck up a conversation, "There is no culture west of our Eastern Seaboard." At this the little old lady tells her vehemently that even our small towns have fine symphonies and fabulous ballet schools which perform Tchaikovsky's Nutcracker Suite every Christmas. Museums and drama companies, colleges and instrumental music teachers. Every town has a Carnegie Library.

Do you know her?

# How the Nuthatch
# Got Its Name

"BOW WOW WOW! What are you doing up in that tree, Sammy Squirrel?" barked Fido. "Bow wow wow! You get right out of there. Wait until Mrs. Gray gets home! I'm going to tell!"

Sammy Squirrel seemed to be eating something good. He smacked his lips, quickly wiped away a drop of something yellow from his chin whiskers, and scurried out to the end of the branch. Nimbly jumping to the next tree, Sammy scampered away, all the while scolding and chattering angrily at Fido for interrupting his mischief.

Just then Mrs. Gray arrived home from her shopping in the mullberry bushes. It was rumored among the neighbors that Mrs. Gray was expecting the arrival of baby birds in her snug little home in the hollow branch of that same tree from which Sammy Squirrel had just been chased. Mrs. Gray looked quickly about to see if everything was just as she had left it. Quickly she hopped through the small round doorway of her home and snuggled down on the six dainty white and brown speckled eggs. They had become quite cool. Mrs. Gray was tired, as it had taken so long to find the things she needed for the expected little ones. Her eggs became warm again, and she fell asleep dreaming about her family.

Next morning tiny peeps awakened Mother Gray as the shells began to crack and five baby birds emerged. "How happy I am," twittered Mrs. Gray. Still, she was anxious about that sixth egg. It didn't want to crack. It showed no signs of cracking. *Well, I'll give it a few more hours to hatch*, she thought.

At eight o'clock Mr. and Mrs. Peck knocked at her door. They called in the window, "Good morning, Mrs. Gray. We thought we'd drop in to see how you're getting along."

"Good morning to you," replied Mrs. Gray. "What pretty black and white suits you're wearing, and how dashing Mr. Peck looks in his bright red cap!"

"Oh, they're old now. We expect to be getting new ones soon," said Mrs. Peck. "Any news?"

"News! Just look here," said Mother Gray raising herself from her downy featherbed to show off her new babies.

"What dears! And so many!"

"Only five," sighed Mother Gray, "and I'm worried about this sixth egg. It just doesn't seem to want to hatch. I can't believe it's mine. Look how brown, and it has a point and feels so hard now that it's the only one to sit upon. Ah, well, I'll try a bit longer. I did promise Mr. Gray there would be six new birdies when he got back from his flight."

"Their Papa will be mighty proud," said Mr. Peck nodding at the little ones. "We must be going but will stop again this afternoon."

They flew over to a dead tree in the next lot. Mr. Peck saw

Sammy Squirrel still chattering and wondered whether he was laughing or scolding. With a rapid tat-tat-too on a hollow tree branch Mrs. Peck called Mrs. Brown Creeper to tell her the news. Jenny Wren in a nearby market bush getting fresh berries heard everything and shook her head doubtfully over that pokey sixth egg. They arranged to call on Mrs. Gray after lunch.

Jenny Wren ate a hurried lunch, put on her brown speckled coat, and straightened her cap. With a hop and a skip, Jenny was ready to fly when Mrs. Peck's tap sounded.

At the Gray home, Mrs. Peck knocked softly and called, "How are you? I brought our neighbor Jenny Wren to see your babies."

"One, two, three, four, five," Mrs. Gray counted as she rose. "I'm so discouraged. I've been sitting for hours. If this pesky egg doesn't hatch soon my babies will starve. I must fetch them something soon."

"You do look blue. Cheer up. I'll ask Red Cardinal to call Dr. Wise Owl," said Mrs. Peck. She flew to the top of a cottonwood tree where Red Cardinal was singing to Mrs. Cardinal several lots away. After hearing the story, Red gave several sharp whistles which echoed across the valley into the deep woods.

Dr. Wise Owl heard the calls, for his ears were very sharp. He blinked, got up and stretched. He usually spent the afternoon snoozing in his big shady oak tree. Several more shrill whistles told him it was an emergency call. Dr. Wise Owl packed his bag, hopped into his airplane, and sailed right over to where Red Cardinal perched. "What's up?" he asked Red.

"Trouble over at the Gray's. A case of irksome duty," said Red with a twinkle in his eye.

"Who?" asked Dr. Wise Owl with a knowing wink.

"I said Mrs. Gray! Can't you hear, you old duffer?" called Red Cardinal.

The doctor blinked but sailed on toward Gray's home in the green ash tree. He heard Jenny Wren scolding Sammy Squirrel for coming too close. Mrs. Peck flattened herself against a dead tree branch and said, "Hello, Dr. Wise Owl. You flew fast. I'll knock for you. Look in carefully. Your big glassy eyes might frighten nervous little Mrs. Gray."

"Ho, ho, ho!" laughed the doctor. "What seems to be the trouble?"

"Dear Doctor, please help me," cried Mrs. Gray. "I've five nice babies born this morning, needing to be fed, but this sixth egg will not hatch." She rose from her nest to show him.

"Let me examine it. Hmp!" said Dr. Wise Owl, adjusting his glasses. "You have a very fine family now and had better begin caring for them. I'll take this odd specimen over to my waiting room for a closer look. My eyesight is poor these days but I can see this does not look right. Jenny Wren, you stay with Mrs. Gray to see that no one disturbs her. Mrs. Peck, you call to your big cousin, Harry, the carpenter with that yellow polka-dotted vest and black apron. Tell him to come quickly and bring his big hammer. You might also call your cousin Red, the redhead, to bring his long electric drill." Mrs. Peck got into her mapleseed glider and hurried to Maple Grove where Cousin Harry the carpenter lived in a comfortable stump left over from the last big windstorm. She hopped to the front door and knocked. Her cousin nearly frightened her off the front porch as he popped his big beak out the window.

"What's the matter?"

"Matter of importance," shouted Mrs. Peck. "There's to be a consultation at Dr. Wise Owl's office in the big oak. He wants you to bring your hammer quickly." Next she found Cousin Red, the Redhead, testing his drill on a hollow branch.

"I'll be right along," said Red, "and I'll bring Bill since he has an electric drill, too." Soon they all dropped into Dr. Wise Owl's office.

"Come in, friends, and solve this problem. Mrs. Gray can't seem to hatch this egg. What's wrong?"

"Let me see," said Harry putting his ear to it, as that was his way of deciding things. "No sign of life. Not a sound."

"Harry, you Yellow Fellow," said Dr. Owl. "I'll hold it on this oak table while you try to crack it with your yellow hammer." Yellow Fellow Harry hammered and hammered but couldn't crack it. "It's no use," said Doctor Owl. "Now, Red, use your drill to see if you can bore into it."

Red got his drill working. Soon he had pieced it, "Umm, it tastes good." He took another bite and began to laugh. "Why, it's not an egg at all! It's a nut!"

Bill picked up a crumb to taste and agreed. "It's our regular daily breakfast food."

Yellow Fellow Harry laughed loudly, "Har, har, har! Won't we have a good joke on Mrs. Gray trying to hatch a nut! From now on we'll call her Mrs. Nuthatch." They all laughed until their sides ached.

"What shall we do with it?" Dr. Owl looked blank for a while.

"Let's take it over to Mrs. Jay Blue's home in the pines and drop it into her nest," said Mrs. Peck. "She likes eggs so let's give her one. Only yesterday I saw her steal an egg from Chickadee's nest and then go about the neigborhood calling, "Thief! Thief!" as if someone else had done it. She even went so far as to suggest Mrs. Cardinal was a-robbin', but Mrs. Cardinal was honest all day. I wouldn't be surprised if Mrs. Jay Blue was the one who put the nut in Mrs. Gray's nest after stealing her egg. I'd like to play this trick on her but I'm so small and her beak is so sharp! Why don't you, Harry?" Harry laughed at the idea of Mrs. J. mistaking a nut for an egg, and was willing to try anything.

"So Mrs. Nuthatch could not hatch her egg," chuckled Dr. Owl. "Go ahead and take it with you. I'm going back to my nap. I may send a bill for deciding this matter."

The birds flocked to Judge Sparrow's porch. He was a smart bird about town, always arguing, talking politics, or giving a bit of legal advice. After hearing their story he said, "Cawsby Crow has been a mean bird. Why not play a joke on him? I see him going to work every morning an hour before I get out for my breakfast, and he doesn't come home until after dark, so he's not home now."

Now the jolly flock flew to Mrs. Nuthatch's house and recited in a gay chorus what a joke it was to try to hatch a nut. They helped her put the nut on a linseed glider and take it to Cawsby Crow's stick and brush nest. No one was at home since all the young crows had grown up and flown. "Will Cawsby be surprised to find an *egg* in his nest!" said Mrs. Nuthatch, slipping the nut into the hollow. They reviewed the whole story noisily and ended in a loud, laughing chorus. Then the birds flew home to their daily chores.

To this day Mrs. Nuthatch can be heard twittering, "Heh, heh,

heh," as she hurries up and down the tree trunks hunting fresh meat. Even Mrs. Peck and her cousin, Bill, can be heard to giggle, and the Flicker to snicker as they think of the joke they played on Cawsby Crow.

# The Horrible Halloween

"FROM SIX UNTIL nine tonight Henry and I want to be at the Masonic Temple Card Party," said Mama phoning Mrs. Zimmerman who lived down North Main from us on Lowell, second house up. "We would feel so much better if your granddaughter could come and help Grace babysit the three little ones." Mary Elizabeth Morman, who'd come to spend a year or two with her grandmother, was twelve years old like Grace. Marjorie, I, and Richie were ten, eight, and six and not too eager to spend a spooky Halloween evening without our parents. Having Mary Elizabeth come over would make it lots of fun.

Mama and Papa told Grace that she and Mary Elizabeth could take us trick-or-treating at five, but we had to stay within sight of the house at all times. Mama decked Richie out in his store-bought Indian suit with fringed arms and legs and a bright red feather headband. Cutting armholes half way down the sides of a pillow case, she slipped me into it, gathering it loosely around my neck with a string. She snipped holes where my eyes and mouth were. Though she tried tucking in the corners, I still resembled a ghost with ears.

For Marjorie, Mama had sewn a padded orange vest with jack-o'-lantern face stitched on, and a tiny green cap. Grace and Mary Elizabeth wore black skirts and helped each other button up black sweaters they had put on backwards so the buttons wouldn't show. They made cardboard cone witches' hats covered with black crepe paper.

At trick-or-treat time it was still light, and we started downhill while Mama and Papa turned uphill toward Madison Park's spiral cement steps going down to the Masonic Temple on Twelfth and Locust. An elderly couple on the corner of Lowell and North Main invited us in for cocoa and gingerbread cat cookies. We said our thanks while they admired our costumes.

Next we headed up Lowell to Grandma Zimmerman's. She had paid Bob Lungwitz and the rest of the Lowell Street gang to rake a huge pile of leaves together (they weren't really a gang but just a bunch of boys.) She passed out two marshmallows apiece to the whole crowd and lit her bonfire, rake in hand to keep it together. We each had to hunt a twig long enough to roast our marshmallows. Once the fire was snapping, crackling, and sending sparks flying upward, we toasted our marshmallows, pulling the sticky gooey mess off to cram into our mouths.

"Wanna go rat-a-tat-tatting with us and soap some windows?" Bob asked Grace and Mary Elizabeth.

Mindful of parental orders, Grace replied importantly, "We're having a Jolly Rogers Buccaneer Pirates Meeting."

Mary Elizabeth chimed in, "There'll be buckets of blood, and brains and eyeballs!" The boys had already made their noise makers - wooden spools carved with notches all around the rims, and string tied and wrapped around the spools so when they held them against people's windows on a pencil and pulled the string, the spools unwound with a dreadful rat-a-tat-tatting. And they had pieces of soap with which to draw faces on people's windows, which seemed infinitely more fun than any old girls' plans, so we parted ways.

We headed uphill to Mrs. Krepps' house, up two flights of steps. She'd be a good source of candy since we often saw her coming home from shopping to put treats into rows of mason jars she kept high on a shelf just inside her cellar door. Now she gave each of us a small bag containing filbert nuts with thick crunchy white coatings, sugary maple leaf candies, Halloway suckers, and gummy orange slices.

Were we brave enough to approach Mr. Keeble's house across the street? We stared apprehensively at Sergeant and Major sitting at attention on either side of Mr. Keeble's front porch steps. Mr. Keeble, the floorwalker at Roshek's Department Store, usually walked home an hour after five o'clock closing time. His two marvelously trained black and white hunting dogs were let out of the fenced-in backyard by his two teen-aged daughters. While the spaniels waited, the girls would sit on the porch swing reading the paper and sipping lemonade. At first sight of Mr. Keeble, Sergeant and Major always lunged down the bank with vociferous hoarse barking to dance frantically around him until he said, "Sit!" Then they'd dash up the bank, long ears flapping, to sit alertly on either side of the steps. When he'd climbed that far, the dogs would recommence bounding around him with their horrific "Arf! Arf!" until he said, "Heel!" Then they'd follow him silently, in single file onto the front porch and through the door.

"Those dogs would never obey us," ventured Grace, "and it's getting dark fast." We hurried home. Mary Elizabeth reminded us, "It's time to fix your Pirate Buccaneer supper. Don't eat any candy until afterward." She shooed us into the dining room to stare at the waiting pumpkin Papa had placed on a tray in the middle of the table. Much giggling behind the closed kitchen door caused us to wonder about the gruesome food they'd promised. Mama had prepared noodles for us, but when the girls invited us into the kitchen, what was on our plates?

"Brains!" said Mary Elizabeth. (They'd added cocoa to make the noodles look different.) It was bitter and made us gag. What next?

"These are just green grapes! You've peeled them!" shouted Marjorie.

"Are you sure green grapes aren't really eyeballs?" asked Mary Elizabeth mysteriously, taking some of the pleasure out of swallowing them.

"Well, you still have to drink the blood," said Grace. She'd put a bottle of red food dye and a slurp of vinegar into our milk. However, that curdled it so even she couldn't drink it. We gleefully poured it down the drain and hurried into the dining room to light the jack-o'-lantern.

Papa had carved a grinning smile, star eyes, and moon earholes so plenty of light shone forth from the big fat candle inside. Mary Elizabeth switched off the lights and we cuddled on the living room sofa watching the light flicker and sway above the jack-o'-lantern casting a weird slanted shadow of the chandelier across the ceiling. The wide wood-framed arch between dining and living room had wooden lattice curlicues in each corner through which unbelievable streaks of light swayed across the living room ceiling.

Mary Elizabeth started telling us a spooky story about the haunting voice that called out every day from blocks away, "I am the viender viper and I'm coming to get you!" Night after night the voice came closer until finally it was right outside the door shouting, "I am the viender viper and I've come to varsh and vipe your vienders!" We were trying to decide whether to scream or laugh when suddenly a strange scritch-scratch sounded in the dark. Everyone shrieked. Total silence fell. Another scritch, scratch, scuttle, scurry.

All five of us leapt over the sofa back and scrunched down trembling. Strange noises crackled in the darkness. Richie started to cry, but Grace put her hand over his mouth. I was petrified, breathless. The canary, which had been covered for the night in his cage in the dining room, suddenly awakened, squawked, and flapped against his bars.

"It's a ghost," whispered Mary Elizabeth in disbelief. Silence followed—emptiness that seemed worse than the noises. We clung together, eyes tight shut, afraid to move, until we fell asleep.

"We're back, children," came Mama's cherry voice. Papa turned on the lights to bedlam as we all rushed to hug them, weeping and wailing, blurting out the frightful noise at the canary cage. When the word canary was uttered, Mama cried out, "Not my lovely canary!" Her hand flew to her breast to calm her breathing.

Papa lifted a corner of the canary's cover and said, "You don't want to look. I'll get some rat traps tomorrow." He gently lifted the cage from its tall stand, carried it out the door, and set it on the porch. We realized we'd heard our lovely canary's death.

"Grace and Mary Elizabeth," said Mama sternly, "having a good scare serves you right for frightening the little ones. Grace and Henry had better escort Mary Elizabeth home now. It's late."

Those big girls clung tightly, one on each of Papa's arms, as he marched them off into the darkness.

# A Shiny Band

WHAT AN ADVENTUROUS life I've led, three times lost, once half-lost, evaluated, cut up and reassembled by professionals, but always treasured—more so every year. Indeed my value can't be measured. I'm admired, gazed upon sentimentally, cared for, handled gently, exclaimed over, even been given my own little nighttime house.

Out of the bowels of the earth I was dug, pounded, sliced, polished, set in hot metal, closed up in a little box, and finally bought by Paul at Sibbing's Jewelry Store in downtown Dubuque.

Life truly began for me in Potterveld's Field behind the University of Dubuque football field. There, surrounded by blossoming apple trees, Paul placed me in the grass saying, "I see something sparkling."

"Oh! A diamond ring ! A gorgeous diamond! Who do you suppose lost it?" exclaimed Ruth.

Paul, ever the jokester, handed her the box I came in saying, "Try it on. Would you like to keep it?"

"Just what I'd hoped for," squealed Ruth. They knocked over the picnic basket in their eager embrace.

That's when I came alive.

I felt a warmth and emotion and a sense of purpose. I'm a circle of hope and promise, a band of loving trust between two people forever together. My diamond is modest but radiant when they let me sparkle in the sun. I looked my very best when, as the wedding band snuggled beside me, I reflected all the lights of St. Luke's from my myriad surfaces.

I have been intimately acquainted with hamburger meatloaf mix, sticky bread dough, dishwater, and once with white ceiling paint which rolled down the brush and so completely doused me that I spent a goodly time in the turpentine jar. Whenever Ruth remembered to take me off the safety of her finger, I was either hung on a cup hook, laid on a narrow ledge behind the kitchen sink, stuffed in a pocket, laid under a pillow, or, most dangerous of all, dropped down an open sink drain from which Paul had to fish me out with a lengthy hooked wire.

Finally Paul bought me my own little house, a tiny round ceramic box with a lid upon which two swans, nestling amid waterlilies, bend their necks toward each other in a heart shape. Every night I'm put here to rest.

This is especially important because Ruth's fingers swell at night. Once when she forgot to take me off, her finger was so painful and purple by morning that I had to be cut in two with a hacksaw blade. That meant a trip to the jewelry store in the mall to be repaired.

The second time I was lost happened back at Potterveld's Field. Because Paul worked nights at John Deere Tractor Works, Ruth had days to fill with adventures. She packed six-month-old DeAda, with a bottle and some sandwiches, into the picnic basket and walked from Finley Street to the apple orchard. After baby was fed and sleeping in the shade, Ruth fell asleep, too, but awoke to feel no rings on her finger. Panic at first, but then she thought, "Where do I usually put them? Right above me on the headboard of the bed." She searched the grass where her head had lain and found me right away.

Half-lost makes an interesting tale. One morning Alice Fuhrman called Ruth on the phone and asked, "When did you become engaged?" Ruth glanced down at me and—horrors!—I was only half there. An ugly empty black spot marked where my diamond should have been.

"Oh, Alice," cried Ruth, "where can my diamond have gone?"

Alice replied, "I once found something miraculously. Maybe you'll have a miracle, too. I walk along Grandview every day from my little white house to Southern Avenue and back, carrying my house key in my hand. One day I had no key when I returned to the house, so I retraced my steps toward the piles of snow at the intersection. Something told me to feel deep down in the snow bank and there was my key. Now I wear it on a long string around my neck. You retrace your steps."

Ruth hung up the phone remembering she'd heard a tiny clink while wiping off the breakfast counter. Then she'd swept the floor. Hurriedly Ruth emptied the kitchen wastebasket and there, amid the dust and crumbs, she found me sparkling.

Another trip to the jewelry store. This time the jeweler explained I needed resetting. "Gold is a soft metal and the prongs holding a diamond get worn away by rubbing against walls, rocks, furniture, or other jewelry. The wedding band and engagement ring should be fastened together to stop friction, and the diamond should be reset in platinum prongs which are more durable. Even then you should check them at times through a magnifying glass." So I came home in better condition than before.

Now I get special care when a magnifying glass shows soap scum has accumulated. Gently I'm brushed with my very own soft toothbrush under hot water (with the drain closed.) Ruth and Paul know I'm their diamond since the jeweler pointed out two infinitesimal carbon flecks on one side, explaining, "Each diamond has its own distinguishing characteristics you should learn to recognize. Yours has a slightly blue tinge, meaning it reflects back to you more of the blue light from the rainbow of colors when it sparkles."

My value to Ruth and Paul has increased because we've been through a lot together. I don't want any more separations, but I'm looking forward to a lot more picnics.

# Black History in Dubuque
# As I Know It

"HOW COME YOU'RE so involved in the N double-A CP?" asked my doctor.

"How can one not be?" I replied. "If anyone of us is neglected, ostracized, hurt or harassed, all of us suffer. Dubuque lately was known as one of the whitest cities in the U.S. with a long history of all these things. However, we started out correctly back in Civil War times by hiding slaves by day in our many caves and mine tunnels as they made their way on the *Underground Railroad* North to freedom."

My first awareness of prejudice came when Mama took us on the excursion boat, *The Capitol*. On the lower deck brother Richard toddled up to a huge black man shoveling coal into the boiler to keep the paddlewheel turning. He innocently smiled, "Hello, Mr. Pickaninny," and received a look of sheer hatred. Quickly Mama pulled away to safety her beautiful blond little boy, realizing he had been dangerously offensive. After that she stopped using her thoughtless expressions like "Pickaninny" and

"Oh, rats and little nigger babies!" when frustrated. She stopped reading us stories like *Little Black Midnight* about a black cat whose soul was washed white.

Mama must have taught us well because I dearly loved my first black acquaintance, Hettie Martin. Hettie was our Girl Reserve counselor at the YWCA who helped us memorize our creed:

> **G**racious in manner
> **I**mpartial in judgment
> **R**eady for service
> **L**oyal to friends
> **R**eaching toward the best
> **E**ager for knowledge
> **S**eeing the beautiful
> **E**arnest in purpose
> **R**everent toward God
> **V**aliant in troubles
> **E**ver dependable, and
> **S**incere at all times.
>
> She lived this creed.

At church Eddie Martin was everyone's favorite. He sang in the choir. Dr. Martin did well as a podiatrist. Mrs. Martin, however, was never made to feel comfortable in our Ladies' Aid Society. They finally left Dubuque, saying there weren't enough people like themselves who their children could choose to date and marry.

Dubuque was not a welcoming town. Since blacks could not

get a marriage license in Illinois, they'd cross the river into Iowa where marriage licenses were legal for everybody. Few stayed because Dubuque didn't offer jobs liberally. Jim Sutton, bravest of the brave, was stationed here by the railroad company. Mean-spirited Dubuquers did everything in their power to get him to leave. They even put rocks and sand in his lunch bucket. Jim endured insults and troubles with patience and courage. His wife, Ruby, started bringing his lunch bucket to him at mealtime.

In 1941 we experienced a rude awakening. Aunt Grace was secretary at the Chamber of Commerce. The popular quartet, *The Ink Spots,* on their national tour appeared in Chicago, with their next scheduled appearance in Dubuque. To Aunt Grace's consternation, no hotel would accept the reservations she tried to make for them. No restaurant would serve them. After hours on the phone, she finally decided she'd host Bill Kenny in her upstairs apartment, their sugary-sweet-voiced high tenor. We'd house downstairs with us Hoppy Jones, who played cello and bass, and sang, and talked his choruses in his deep intimate bass voice. The other two office girls agreed to house Deek Watson, second tenor, and Charlie Fuqua, baritone and guitar. Aunt Grace was embarrassed as she explained the makeshift arrangements to them, but we had a gala dinner with them and then went to the Grand Theater to hear them.

Dubuquers loved the Ink Spots on stage. They sang *"If I Didn't Care"* and the audience clapped a bit. They sang *"I Don't Want to Set the World on Fire"* and everyone really clapped. By the time they sang *"We Three, My Echo, My Shadow, and Me,"* cheers and stamping reinforced our clapping. Their *"When the Swallows Come Back to Capistrano"* evoked warmth in the audience and

*"I'm Getting Sentimental over You"* moved some to tears. *"My Prayer"* and *"I'll Never Smile Again"* brought down the house. As the final curtain dropped, folks turned their backs upon them. Even the stagehand's cold stares said, "You can sing, sure, but we don't want you here, get back on that train. You don't belong here."

Mr. Ferdinand DiTella, our band director at High School, was truly mortified at Dubuque. He himself had received many a slight and snub in this Irish and German town, simply because he was Italian and looked it. Mr. Di opened up a restaurant right across from the Grand Theater and put up a big sign in the window: "We Serve Everybody." Alas, Mr. Di, who had diabetes, died shortly thereafter. The friendly sign was removed from his restaurant by the next owner.

I recall being stymied about how to help Mr. Steene find a job when he moved here from the South. Interstate Power would hire him to shovel coal only if he filled out a lengthy and hard to read application form. Though he could shovel coal, he couldn't fill out the form. He moved his family to California.

When Sugar Ray and Cynthia Sanders graduated from the University of Dubuque, their home was subjected to criminal mischief and their garage was set on fire. That's when I saw the need for active participation.

The black population in Dubuque was at 1%. Although 10% of the country was black. As black people moved to Dubuque, jobs were seldom offered. Our three colleges have bent over backwards to introduce all races into the student body and give cosmopolitan exposure to this very backward and provincial town. Drum circles, talk circles and neighborhood activities developed friendships. While newspapers were quick to capitalize on violence and unrest, they also increased their coverage of our attempts to create peace and harmony.

The first Dubuque Chapter President, Ernestine Moss, and Police Chief John Mauss led the city council to accept a Memorandum of Understanding between the police, the city, and the NAACP. Arguments, fights, misdemeanors between black and white needed dispute resolution and mediation rather than going straight to police and jail.

In 1988 the annual Freedom Fund Banquet put on by the local NAACP began bringing in noteworthy speakers such as Julien Bond, Dick Gregory, Merlie Evers, and Bishop Thomas, the first black Methodist bishop in Iowa. It has also recognized annually with the Ruby Sutton Award, people who have advanced understanding between races.

John Deere Tractor Works has hired minorities, as have medical and school professions, city and government offices. Thomas Determan, Director of Equity Operations in the Dubuque Community School District, along with Ernestine Moss, has run for over 15 years the annual Martin Luther King Essay Contest in both public and parochial schools. By encouraging students to research the contributions different races have made to the fabric of our national life, better attitudes and understanding among the student bodies has been promoted.

High Student Achievement, Collaboration, and Equity/ Diversity have been the established goals of our school district since 1992. This sent a message to parents, pupils, and patrons that diversity and integration are steppingstones to peaceful progress.

In restaurants and hotels our color bar has been lowered or

removed. A lawsuit or two have nudged realtors and landlords to extend equal housing opportunity. Exclusively white churches have become inclusive under the leadership of Dubuque Area Congregations United. What people couldn't or wouldn't do alone, they have achieved together. We've seen the entrance of Hispanic, Bosnian, Vietnamese, Mariana Islanders, and other ethnic groups into our neighborhoods. It's an embarrassment to be all white anymore.

Who's keeping score? If this once whitest of white cities can grow thus far, so can other smaller cities like us.

# A Shiny Bit of Lead

FROM OUR ORDINARY clapboard house on the hill we viewed an ordinary world until Papa bought the six-volume set of *Bookhouse.* Even the black, white, gold, and pale orange illustrations, some of them by Maxfield Parrish, kindled our dreams. Nightly we four piled upon my bed as Mama read one story for each of us—fairy tales for me, animal and adventure stories for Marjie, and myths, legends, and biographies, for Grace. By the time Grace's stories rolled around, Richie was always asleep.

However, the stories that made us squirm and tremble were those told by Louise, the hired girl who took care of us. She coerced us into good behavior by warning us about the Creekeldys in the attic, the Darkeldings in the cellar, and the Whumpelboos under our beds.

"You'd better get to sleep right this minute," she threatened, tucking us in for our naps. I was determined to investigate her veracity. As soon as she left the room, I leaned way over the bed, holding onto the mattress while my head hung down, staring into the dark until my brain felt woozy. Gradually a little green bewhiskered man appeared.

"Are you a Whumpelboo?" I whispered.

"I'm Wembeldy Jackeldy," he whispered back, "and I know you. You're the girl who always loses one sock under this bed." He proceeded to drag it out and place it upon the other sock by my shoes at the bedside. Then he whirled about rounding up Richie's marbles and my jacks in between sweeping up dust bunnies and patting them into little cushions just his size.

"You really are a Wembeldy Jackeldy," I giggled watching his whirling red and white barber pole socks propelling him about his cleaning up business with dizzying speed.

"All straight. Let's go," said Wembeldy Jackeldy, brushing his hands together. He sprang to the windowsill, slid down a sunbeam, and disappeared in the sun-baked lawn below. I jumped up and slid after him.

"Where are you?" I called and he grabbed my hand. How very weird! Either he'd grown taller or I'd grown smaller, for Wembeldy Jackeldy and I were now the same size and suddenly cooler in the tall grasses towering over us.

"Stay off the path, and watch out for ants," he cautioned. The path loomed wide and there loomed even larger shiny black ants with huge, pincer-like legs. "This will keep them busy," said Wembeldy Jackeldy, drawing from his baggy pocket a piece of cheese to place in the path. We fled between grass stems and hurried on by.

"Mama said *never* to go on this path between the gardens," I hesitated, but Wembeldy Jackeldy pulled me along. The sound of Mr. Hanover on the left hoeing his beans was a gigantic earth-shaking thud. I heard his sister's sweet voice calling him to lunch, but high and hollow like a faraway yawning echo. On the right crazy Matt Thimish, a towering giant drunkenly swaying at the top of the cement steps, was shaking his fist and swearing in a thunderous rumble at the distant sound of cars honking down on Central Avenue. His sister was screaming at him to come inside and be quiet. Droning of the cicadas was a shrieking buzzsaw against hardwood. Crow calls split the sky.

Wembeldy Jackeldy led me into the woods, promising it would be quieter. What fun walking beside him! Every few steps he'd hop and skip. It must have been because of his twirling socks that kept winding him up. Suddenly there stood Mr. Badger in his rich brown fur coat. He had mean teeth and claws, and beady glittering eyes. "You're late for work!" he growled, stepping aside so we could go through a crack in a large mound of rocks, which turned out to be the entrance to a cave. It instantly shut out the heat and noise, but there was a humming of the very earth, a singing and a sighing of the depths. Light filtered through cracks of the rock pile above and glinted on the metalic streaks here and there enough to light our way. We followed tunnels slanting down, down, down.

"Where are we?" I ventured, but was reassured to see a rabbit poke his nose out.

"You're well below the burrows of the mice and moles, the foxes and snakes. I've just come down for a long cool run." He scampered ahead where increasing light shimmered. Turning a corner, I gasped at a wonderland of rainbow-hued crystal walls with crazy angles, strange shapes wedged one against another from ceiling to floor.

"It's like being in a watercolor geode," I sighed. About the cavern floated haunting vibrations of soothing tones with no particular tune to them.

"Earth melody," explained Wembeldy Jackeldy. "This is our crystal room. Do you like it?"

"It's about time you showed up," came a querulous voice out of a pile of purple plush. Here was another bewhiskered little green man shaking himself awake and stretching until little gold buttons popped off his purple waistcoat and one by one plopped into bowls of steaming mashed potatoes, gravy, and green peas laid out on a gleaming glass table before him. "There, that ought to do it," he declared, pulling off the remaining gold button and dropping it into a glass of sparkling water. "Will you sup with me while he's off to work?" he asked, raising his glass to guzzle noisily.

"If you please, I'd better stay with Wembeldy Jackeldy. Wait for me," I called and caught up to him. We approached a deep hole.

"This is the mine shaft," said my little friend helping me climb into a slatted box hanging from a pulley supported by a tripod of heavy beams. Stout ropes attached to a windlass were slowly lowering us deep down a dark shadowy narrow shaft past huge layered blocks of cool, damp, musty-smelling limestone. Deep, deep down we went until my ears pounded and green and pink twinkles danced in the dark within my own eyes. We bumped to a stop. Gradually I could make out little gray men in the dark cavern winding the ropes on pegs to stop our descent, then reaching out to help us out of the slatted box. Mystery upon mystery! I could see right through them as they moved about. Wembeldy Jackeldy zipped along a passage lighting tiny headlamps on a row of miners' caps. Each miner was standing with left hand on the right shoulder of the miner ahead of him so they wouldn't get lost in the dark. With their lamps now relieving the darkness, they separated and went cheerfully about their work hacking at the rocks with pickaxes, loading buckets with their findings, and heaving them into carts on a low set of rails running through the mine. They were shades of their former selves; shadowy miners softly whistling through their teeth, moving eerily before me, but in no way shutting off the view of pearly white stalactites hanging from the cavern ceiling and piles of yellowed or grayish white stalagmites building up into peaks on the ground below. The rocks they'd chopped from the limestone were jumbles of milky quartz, clear quartz, rose quartz, fool's gold, and gleaming square chunks of lead growing one square against another in tumbled formation.

"I've done what I came to do. We can go home now," exclaimed Wembeldy Jackeldy, pulling me into the slatted box once more while signaling a shadowy ghost of a miner to pull the ropes. I snatched a rock from the rail cart as we speedily rose upward. My head suddenly felt a hard bump.

"Sweetheart," cooed Louise, "you fell out of bed and hit your head." She swept me up in her arms and carried me into the bathroom to bathe my forehead with cold water. "See how your hair is standing up on end. You look like you've seen a ghost," she laughed as she smoothed my black bangs down toward my eyebrows.

"I did. I saw a lot of ghosts," I said soberly.

"You were having a bad dream, sweetheart," Louise laughed. "There are no ghosts. You mustn't believe all the ghost stories I tell."

But I knew what I'd seen. Besides, I knew the real name of the little fellow living under my bed. Peeking at the shiny bit of lead still clutched in my hand, I secreted it in my pocket.

# Red, White, and Blue Christmas

"'DECK THE HALLS with Boughs of Holly' is my favorite carol because it's so happy," says six-year-old Chris as we start draping an evergreen garland atop the 30-by-40-inch oil copy painting Grandpa Herrmann did of George Washington crossing the Delaware on Christmas Eve. "Tell it again. Where's Grandpa Sala?"

Judson, eleven years old, finishes taping the garland as we stand back to take a look. "Well, Jacob Sala was your great grandfather seven generations back. You can't see him in this picture because he's on this side of the Delaware where we're standing. That's George Washington out there coming to get him."

"Why is it so dark?" asks Christian, tracing his finger over the blue-black waters, the soldiers with long poles pushing the boats through gray chunky ice, the pale streak of gold barely lighting the dawn sky.

"And what is Grandpa Sala doing?"

"He's singing 'Stillege Nacht.' That's 'Silent Night' in German.

You see, he was a Hessian soldier hired to fight for the British. General Howe had quartered his troops in cabins for the winter. They were celebrating and singing, never dreaming that Washington would come in the dark on Christmas Eve across a dangerous river to attack."

"What's a Hessian soldier?"

"They made up one third of King George's British forces trying to make us rebellious colonists give up when we were fighting for freedom. Thirty thousand Germans were sold into British forces by their monarchs. Seventeen thousand of these were from Hesse-Kassel. They were called Hessians."

"Did Granpa Sala get shot?"

"No. George Washington, with only three thousand exhausted soldiers of his own, had shrewdly destroyed or seized all the boats along the Delaware to stall the British, then surprised and overwhelmed the vastly larger Hessian force. He was smart enough to give those Hessians the choice of being shot or deserting the British and joining his Colonial forces. Grandpa Sala along with thousands of Hessians knew a good choice when it was offered. They joined the Continental Army and helped win the Revolution."

"One of your grandfathers was named Eli Morgan Sala because Jacob Sala fought under General Morgan. After the war Jacob brought his family to America and his son, Jacob Otto Sala, became a doctor and married Magdalene, General Morgan's younger sister. Lucky for you boys they didn't all stay in Germany."

Annually the Ham House Museum drapes red and green up its stair railings and across its doorframes. Cinnamon spice wafts through its hallways in a Victorian Christmas Celebration. Our children always flock to the Civil War room where a Christmas tree is somberly decorated with tiny red, white, and blue flags. They remember another Christmas story I've told them of Grandma Campbell having to wait through four Christmas holidays until her young brother finally came home.

Otto Sala, Grandma Mattie Sala Campbell's fifteen-year-old brother, was a dashing young cavalryman who fought in the Civil War, mustering out at age nineteen. Many were the teenagers from Dubuque County and Grant County in Wisconsin who volunteered while mature men worked the farms and supplied the troops, while even old men volunteered for guard duty or wherever needed. The young men, boys really, could ride bareback and shoot varmint, wildcats, foxes, and wolves with a shotgun to protect the farm livestock. They knew how to use guns.

Otto Sala was in the First Iowa Cavalry, Company A, at the 1862 battle of Prairie Grove, Arkansas, along with many of the Grant County boys of the twentieth Wisconsin Infantry. They fought with General Herron's 3,300 troops near Springfield, Mo. General Blunt's 5,000 men had been driving out rebels of Northwest Arkansas. When Confederate General Hindman gathered 25,000 troops and attacked, General Herron's army resisted savagely. Blunt's army heard the firing and joined the defense. Together they forced the rebels South. The quality of these young Iowa and Wisconsin men and boys as they marched into the line of fire, left half of them dead or wounded because they held their ground and wrenched a grim victory over the Southerners, deciding much for the Union. It brought into the Union 100,000 Missourians and 7,000 Arkansans who were wavering. It sent into the battlefield thousands of men from neighboring states who would have stayed at home. It helped General Grant secure the Ohio and Mississippi River valleys from Confederate expansion. But it made a red, white, and blue Christmas for so many homes.

More recent Christmas memories date to 1942, during World War 11. Coming back after Christmas holidays, we felt the haunted emptiness in our school halls because so many classmates had enlisted over New Year's Day. The culmination was realizing old Bulldog Johnson, our principal, was human after all, and cared for us. When we trooped across the stage at graduation to shake his hand and receive our certificates, he had to pause and wipe his glasses each time he'd read, "James Carney, died in the service of his country, . . . Chuck Doran, died in the service of his country, . . . Don Dolphin, died in the service of his country . . ." So many died between Christmas and graduation time. Patriotism, adds blue to the red and white of Christmas.

Sometimes it's funny memories at Christmas. Consider the traditional fruitcake gift. I gave many a lousy fruitcake, either burned or underdone, too much batter, not enough batter, even gone high from home-made fruit compote. The classic which I sent to Cousin Robert, serving on the battleship *Missouri* in the South Pacific, could have started another war. I'd mailed it three months early to assure timely delivery, even packed it in popcorn to prevent crushing.

"Don't send fruitcake ever again!" wrote Bob. "It was a solid block of mold from the heat of the ship's hold. We couldn't even eat the popcorn for the smell!" It's not for sentimental reasons that I no longer send fruitcake to anyone.

# Let Catfish
# Creek Be Dammed

ALONG THE BANKS of Catfish Creek, the large mound of a beaver lodge camouflaged in pristine snow was revealed only by faint steam rising from its top in the pre-dawn hush. Bud Beaver, opening a dreamy eye to peer up through the center opening of his sleeping chamber, thought the loosely woven branches etched against a burgeoning blush of pink and gold streaked sky looked like a fifteen-inch rose window. Sleepily Bud shoved 2-year-old Little Bud off his back, counted with his feet the yearlings Buford, Byron, and Bonnie snuggling there. Bud rolled closer to Beatrix Beaver saying, "Are you awake? Care for a little swim?"

"If you go, I'll go, but what about the little ones? Come on, kids, everybody out. We like to keep a clean house." She chased them down off the excelsior bed of fine wood strips onto the eating and grooming platform ten inches below their bedroom. "Everybody oil up well before getting into the water, and comb that fur!" They all sat on their flat oval tails and rubbed creamy yellow waterproofing oil from their castoreum glands between their legs onto their shoulders, bellies, faces, and everywhere reachable with their little forepaws. Beavers are covered all over with sleek two-inch stiff reddish brown guard hairs under which they bear soft, dense, warm three-quarter-inch dark brown fur. The guard hairs have minute scales arranged in over-lapping pattern like shingles. They constantly must comb and oil their fur to resist water and cold. Their webbed hind feet have two split toenails to aid in this combing.

Beavers are truly beautiful furry rodents, *Castor Canodensis,* descended from *Casteroides,* a pre-historic beaver weighing eight hundred pounds, large as a black bear at eight feet long with a fourteen-inch skull. Bud, a modern four-year-old, was only fifty inches long and weighed eighty pounds, though someday he might weigh a hundred. Beatrix, his beautiful mate, was slightly smaller. They were monogamous, mating for life. If she died, he would batch it the rest of his days, but if he died, she might seek another mate.

"Just look at our eldest. Little Bud is already nine inches at the shoulder and weighs thirty-five pounds. The yearlings are only thirteen pounds and still need us parents," said Bea.

"What was that?" exclaimed Big Bud, perking up his very keen tiny ears. They all imitated him. It was the January 19th thaw. A thick fog was billowing upcreek from the Mississippi, a warming trend. Three slender-legged deer had picked their way daintily to the bank and the buck slammed his hoof into a thin spot of ice, breaking a hole for fresh water. Where the Catfish runs four feet deep, it freezes two feet down, but thin spots show where underwater springs of fifty-six degrees bubble up. Beaver will only come out through these holes onto snow banks when the temperature is above sixteen degrees. Skunk cabbage with an internal heat of seventy-six degrees pushes up even through January's ice and snow, and might tempt them out for the first fresh food of the winter.

All winter beavers fetch sapling branches from their supply stashed underwater right outside their lodge burrows, bringing twigs inside onto the platform four inches above water line to strip and chew the bark. Lignite of the inner wood they cannot digest, so these bare sticks are saved for springtime reinforcement of their lodge. The exit and entry burrows are in the creek bank underwater because most of their enemies cannot swim beneath the surface. Five tunnels have been dug providing quick escape should a predator try to dig into their thick-branched, darkened, mud-cemented lodge.

"It's only deer. Let's go," commanded Bud, and all scrambled down and out of their burrows, their four rows of three-inch long whiskers helping them avoid the walls.

"You're built to swim," smiled Beatrix fatuously as her progeny glided into the water. They all swam twenty feet downstream to void body wastes and return home. For underwater swimming their valvular nose and ears close. Nictating membranes close over their eyeballs as underwater goggles. They stay submerged five minutes, but are able to stay down fifteen. They breathe in air pockets between ice and water. Their heartbeat slows, conserving oxygen for the brain. Their large lungs hold more air and can exhale at least seventy-five percent of capacity compared to a human's twenty percent. Their large liver stores more oxygenated blood. They can swim half a mile submerged.

"I see the deer's water hole! Let's climb out for greens!" shouted
Little Bud.

"Not before dark, or the fox or bobcat will get you. Or maybe
black bear, lynx, cougar, otters, or wolves. We can't fight them but
we can hide. We're safer at night," explained Big Bud, leading
them home.

"Everyone pull in your own branches and start chewing before
those incisors get too long," lectured Mama Bea. As they came
through the burrow entrances pulling their saplings in their
mouths, butt end first, she lined them all up on the lower platform to shake water from their ears and fur, to drip dry and to
eat their aspen, alder, or willow bark. Mama Bea admired their
rows of four large incisor teeth each, coated with tough bright
orange enamel caused by the iron in their diet. She busily set a
good example grinding top teeth against bottom, which eventually causes all beaver incisors to take on a chisel shape.

Though their forepaws have no opposable thumbs, their five
stout long-nailed toes are very facile at holding and rolling twigs
like ears of corn as they strip the bark one inch at a time. Their
molars grind up about three pounds of inner and outer bark a day
to answer nutritional needs and build up insulation fat. Though
they have large stomachs, beavers eat so much bulk some of it
passes through undigested, so they eat it again to absorb more
nutrients—like most rodents, beavers are *coprophagous*. Fat is
even stored in their tails.

"Your tails are inherited from our pre-historic ancestors; all
black and leather scales with cross-hatched lines," said Bud. "Eat
up while I tell you a story. Once there were beaver lodges from
sea to sea. Your great, great, great grandparents were killed by

the Indians to trade beaver pelts for white man's metal tools and pots. The French trapped them for fur coats. Your great grandparents were trapped by the British for fur hats. Their pelts were soaked and pounded until the scales interlocked, making handsome durable beaver hats. Your grandpas' skins were even boiled for glue. Luckily for us the silk top hats came into favor before we were all killed off. These days we beavers build dams in National Parks where we ought to be safe, but farmers and road crews have hunted down and wrecked every dam I've tried building."

"Why do they hate us, Pa?"

"Because we can build dams that are engineering marvels."

"I'll show them!" piped up Little Bud. I'm only two years old and thirty-five pounds and I have no tools, but I can build the best damn dam ever! I'll change Catfish Creek to a huge pond. It will flood crops, roads, timber, highways, and railroad culverts. No other animal can beat me at changing the environment. Road crews and farmers may break down my dam but I'll keep on rebuilding."

"Pipe down and go to sleep," scolded Ma Bea, leading them all up to the bedchamber to continue the regimen of twenty-eight hours of sleep at a stretch until the second thaw would reset their biological clocks to a higher metabolic rate for mating.

"How about it, Bea?" asked Bud embracing her.

"Shall we have a spring birth? April, May, or June sometime."

"Things are getting too crowded," complained Little Bud. "I'm out of here."

"Be off, already," muttered his preoccupied parents. "Find a mate, build your own place, and let the Catfish Creek be dammed." They gave him a shove.

March 21st is the spring equinox. Early March snowmelt advances north fifteen miles a day. Icy ponds thaw. At thirty-two degrees grasses push up. At forty-four degrees aspen, willow and alder buds swell and burst. Rhizomes, leaves, flowers of white and yellow pond lilies are eagerly eaten. Beavers hunger for grasses, sedges, ferns, flags, fungi, berries, mushrooms, duckweed, and warm water algae. They gorge on everything.

Back at the lodge, Bud said, "Bea, I'll leave for a few days to give you some privacy. Now Byron, Buford, and Bonnie, be good and help your mother out." Flustered father fled. Eagerly the yearlings named the new kits Betty, Bobby, Bernice, and Bradley, each twelve inches, fully furred, open-eyed and eared, incisors bursting (white gradually turning orange), and knowing how to swim, but unable to dive and get out of the burrow for three weeks, after which they'd be weaned. These little kits were spoiled rotten by their overly attentive siblings who carried and played with them, groomed them, brought them so much fresh food that the kits whined a lot, even barking for more. Mother continued to groom them for three weeks. At two months they could sit up on their tails, groom themselves, and debark a twig.

Beaver eyes, ears, and nose are all located atop their skulls, enabling them to swim deeply hidden, but watching, listening and smelling for any danger. They swim with webbed hind feet spread six inches wide moving in unison, while moving their tails in an up-and-down motion to propel them forward. Their forefeet are balled into little fists held at their chests while swimming, sometimes pushing aside floating objects. While floating, their tails act as stabilizers as they feed on foliage and strip off bark. A fur flap covers space between front incisors and back molars to keep wood chips and water from entering their mouths during underwater cutting.

Big Bud checked out his lodge, digging new burrows. He used forepaws to tunnel slanting upward to the lodge. Hind feet pushed the dirt out. Every five or ten minutes he had to surface for air. Next he began expanding and reinforcing the lodge to accommodate his growing family. Pulling long sticks stripped of bark vertically up the outside of the lodge, using bare sticks from last year's feeding stash to pin them in place, he then coated all of it in mud.

"Time to teach the kits to dive underwater and come out to feed," said Bud. Beavers keep alert, pausing often to scan, listen, and sniff for predators. Their smelling sense is a hundred times more sensitive than ours, and their auditory canal as big as ours, though the outside looks small.

Accustomed to living in the dark, they still see well and have remarkable spatial memory and maze-like maps in their brains. Their loud powerful tail slaps warn beavers on land to dash for water, those in the shallows to head for deeper water, and to parade back and forth on guard. Baby beaver tail slaps are just practice. Babies hiss when angry. They churrrr when threatened, and give a prolonged ooooh when content.

Bonnie, Byron, and Buford amused their parents by showing off for the kits, in a Walt Disney cartoon of a dance upright in the shallows swaying back and forth, play wrestling, pushing, kicking like mad, and diving like synchronized porpoises.

Busiest of all were Little Bud and his mate, Bo Peep. Choosing trees which would fall where they planned to dam, hers smaller than his, they sniffed for safety, stood on hind legs holding their front legs against the trees. They sniffed the bark, turned their heads sideways, held upper teeth solidly against the trees, opened their lower jaws wide, masseter muscles forcing teeth through the bark and wood at a forty-five degree cut. Next they held their heads upside down to make a lower cut of forty-five degrees. These two cuts equaled the efficient ninety-degree angle humans strive for when chopping down a tree. While Little Bud continued around his tree quickly cutting chips at both ends and tearing them loose, making each succeeding cut smaller, Bo Peep made all her cuts on the uphill side of the tree. As Little Bud's tree fell, she pushed hers over. Madly they dashed to the water to avoid the falling trees and see if any predators had heard and come to investigate. Now all the beavers came to feed on the leaves.

All helped Little Bud and Bo now cut brush upstream to tow by mouth, butt end first, and push these, with their powerful jaws and shoulders, into the creek bottom. They wove in more brush until a layer spanned the creek, pushing rocks into the dam base to weigh down the brush. With forepaws and chin they held and carried cornstalks, sticks, mud, and rocks to the site while walking upright. Even the little ones dragged a twig or two. Into this anchored layer they pushed one-inch sticks as fasteners. They packed on brush, poles, logs, butt ends downstream. Gradually mud and debris clogged the holes and caused Catfish Creek to rise. Adding more building material, always using the water level as guide to keep the dam even, now they used their teeth to push and pull larger sticks, logs, and poles over the top of their dam and slid them down the other side to reinforce the dam downstream, making a thirty-degree scalene triangle. Hoover Dam copies this formula. The upstream face was one and a half times longer, which greatly strengthened it.

"Mighty fine piece of work there, youngsters," said Big Bud. "Now what you need to do is build an auxiliary dam downstream to back water up against the base, reducing pressure. You want just enough water to flow through, but not too much. And you can build your own lodge right out in the middle of your pond. You must check it every evening, repair it, heighten it, or extend it."

"Da-ad!" complained Little Bud. "All I want is to go for a swim now." He didn't reckon on the angry farmers, the railroad crews, or the flash floods, but they came! Little Bud said, "Damn it."

# Anatomy of a Song

THESE HILLS GIVE birth to enduring melody. The trees lean to hear the tune, then toss and sway, caught up in its rhythm. The road's twists and turns let the song repeat itself. Each bend and rise lets the notes soar free to tumble downhill in harmony. It isn't just the humming tires or whistling breeze. Music lies here in the valleys of the earth rising up to all who listen. Consider the anatomy of a song.

One of my melodies burst straight out of Dodge Street before its many twists were straightened, its high points lowered, and its low spots raised to moderate the roller coaster effect. My students produced the words haphazardly. "What we need is an American Band, the Red, White, and Blue Band," enthused George Wittstock who excelled in divergent thinking. I had my 8th grade Washington Junior High School Special Education class spend the last five minutes before closing bell reviewing for me what they had learned in Social Studies Class so, hopefully, it would be remembered.

"We haven't any blue people," sneered Bill, "and Jimmy

Walking Bear isn't really red, and I'm sure not white, more like pink."

"And I'm not so black, sorta tan color," spoke up Edward. "There'd have to be some yellow people, too."

"Where did we all come from, and why?" I asked.

"From all over the world, to make a new start, a United States," answered Jenny.

"It's a wonder we're united the way we all look and act so different," laughed Bill.

"But don't you see, it has to be all one country. We can look and work different alongside each other. I can have just as good a chance as the rest of you," insisted Jenny. "We ought to stand up for freedom altogether."

"Yeah! We fought a lotta wars to make the United States, not just playin' a dumb old band," declared Ed. The dismissal bell rang. As they filed out, I mused over their discussion. I straightened my room, collected and finished materials for the next day, locked the trailer door, and went to my car in the back parking lot.

As I drove to a stop at the Lombard Street exit, a tune started in the air. *United we stand.*

Proceeding on Lombard to Dodge Street stop sign, I sang *the American band,* traffic slowed. I swung left onto Dodge. *From all over the world,* stop sign on Grandview Avenue, *To carve out a new land.* I tested my brakes for the steep incline as the tune descended the scale. *With an axe or a bow, or a musket in hand,* I slowed for the curve at Booth Street. *We'll let everyone know it's for freedom we stand.* I slowed for Bryant and a full stop. A sharp angle brought a change of pace and melody as Dodge smoothed out into a long gentle slant. Catching sight of leafy woods on the right leading up to that glorious river view from Cleveland Park, I sang, *Oh, don't you see it's meant to be, all one country from sea to sea. Beyond every hill there's another new thrill, and behind every tree, forests stretch endlessly.* Passing the little old doll's hospital on the left huddled under the Mercy Hospital bluff, I smiled as Jenny's words came to me. Rhythm changed with the sharp right turn onto the flat. *There's room in this country for you and for me.*

Full stop and the light turned green as I swung triumphantly onto South Locust. *It's America, land of the free.* Where George's faded green clapboard house leaned against the huge flat-faced fallen rock, I shifted waiting to turn into the Sears parking lot. *Raise the red, white, and blue flag.* Into the parking lot I sailed on the wings of my song, and slid to a stop, my trip accomplished. *Forevermore we stand for freedom, my country and me.* Turning off the ignition, I echoed softly *Wave the red, white, and blue flag. Forevermore she will be tied fast to you and to me.*

In the silence, I realized an entire melody had wafted up from these hills. In order to hold onto it, I must repeat it immediately. A second verse would save it. *United we stand, the American band, red, white, yellow, black, tan. All the world in this land. Where a woman's her own, and a man is a man. Everyone has a chance. We've a share in the plan.* Locking the car, I headed for Sears's back entrance singing, *Oh, don't you see, it has to be all one country from sea to sea.* Entering I passed by plumbing fixtures. *We can all drink our fill where the waterfalls trill.* I turned right toward gardening supplies and tools. *If we dig our hoe deep rich the fruits we can reap.*

Everyone was staring at me so I returned to the bathroom fittings whispering my chorus determinedly. *There's room in this country for you and for me. It's America, land of the free. Raise the red, white, and blue flag.* I didn't even recognize my own face staring at me out of the mirror in the washstand display unit as I mouthed *Forevermore we stand for freedom, my country and me.* Rushing outside to the fresh air, I finished softly singing, *Wave the red, white, and blue flag. Forevermore she will be tied fast to you and to me.* Who was I? A composer who'd just created a song? No, I was just someone who'd caught one of the melodies burgeoning up from these richly verdant hills.

# How Dubuque Got an Ice Harbor

*Pursuit, Place, Profit, Persistence, and Partnership* made possible the Ice Harbor at Dubuque. Julien Dubuque *pursued* lead back in 1778 by living peacefully with his French Canadians among the Indians and acquiring grants from Indians and the Spanish governor to mine lead to sell in St. Louis. The *Place* was significant, midway between St. Louis and St. Paul, midway between Lake Michigan and the Missouri River, and in direct line from Chicago.

**1828** – *The Galena* was the first steamboat to land here and trade for *profitable* lead from Indians after Julien died. Much of Dubuque, especially the south end, was then a swamp. White men mined here before the Black Hawk War treaty made it legal. They created a miner's permit of 200 square yards of land to mine for lead. They were chased out by government troops.

**1832** – Miners returned. Settlers were allowed in and the 200-square-yard land permits the miners had already agreed

upon were followed. They erected furnaces, stockpiling their
lead until spring when navigation was possible. Men canoed
across the Mississippi, and enterprising settlers followed.
Farming and lumbering of oak, maple, ash, walnut, and pine
were added to the lead mining industry. A wagon shop
opened up. Chicago had to turn its swamps like ours into
land by lining its lake banks with rock and filling in ground.
Only gradually was our shoreline shoved outward as dredging spewed sand fill from Jones Street north, building up our
waterfront into more solid useable land. From 1837 on there
are council records of very active men *persisting* to make this
useable waterfront out of the tortured sloughs and swamps of
the Mississippi at Dubuque by dredging a deep channel and
using the spoil for solid fill.

**1835** – General George Wallace Jones, hero of the Blackhawk
War, procured the grant of 640 acres for Dubuque and worked
vigorously to pass the bill establishing Iowa Territory. He had
built the first reverberating lead-smelting furnace in Iowa. While
a U.S. Senator, he signed the Homestead Act so settlers rather
than land speculators would have fair opportunities. Jones procured railroad land grants, which invited immigration, labor, and
wealth into Dubuque and Iowa. He eventually secured the extension of the Illinois Central Railroad into Dubuque.

**MARCH 1837** – An act of Congress entitled towns to sell off
public lands and apply the proceeds to improvements such as our
waterfront. Business and hopes prospered.

**APRIL 1837** – Removing river obstructions and hiring men
to change the flooding watercourse from the ravine would make
a more direct channel to the Mississippi. A dredge was hired.

**1838** – Taxes were levied on steamboats to pay for this dredge. City taxes that year were about $5 on 99 persons or businesses, for a total of $524.

**JUNE 1839** – The town engineer was instructed to set the grade for long wharves stretching 100 feet from Main Street to the 4th Street intersection. Some of the town was under water at floodtide.

**AUGUST 1839** – Contracts were let for embankment from lower landing where Main Street intersects 4th, the base to be 21 feet and top 15 feet wide. City now collected $645 taxes from 123 firms and individuals.

**SEPTEMBER 1840** – At a special meeting Congress gave to Dubuque the net proceeds from the sale of the land on which the town sat to enable Dubuques in our corporate capacity to improve the town's streets and long wharves.

**MAY 1841** – Improvement of the harbor was put under supervision of the Street Commissioner to open a canal connecting the inner and outer sloughs, and to add a levee on the town side to make a good steamboat landing. Major Booth won and lost more money than anyone in Dubuque. Booth was a lawyer and banker who sold land warrants and, along with Captain Barney, surveyed and speculated on land until the crash of '57. Booth had the first steam engine in Dubuque running his lumber mill.

**JUNE 10, 1841** – Water became sufficiently low for Mr. Dougherty to work the dredge, deepening the channel. He was paid $4.

**JUNE 14, 1841** – $500 paid to Dougherty. Also Peter Drake contracted to dig 400 feet on the south end of town at 25¢ a square yard. A. McDaniel was paid to dig 300 feet on the north end at 35¢ a square yard.

**AUGUST 1841** – Large islands between the main river channel and our waterfront prevented steamboats at low water from approaching our wharves. $1000 more was ordered appropriated, as $3500 had now been spent on the canal.

**MAY 1842** – City Council Committee drafted a letter to Congress asking them to donate to the city the islands opposite Dubuque, thus promoting *partnership* and progress.

**DECEMBER 1844** – Harbor Committee sent a reminder to Congress that Dubuque was waiting upon Captain Barney to survey the Harbor of Dubuque. Congress appropriated $7500. (Captain Barney, dredge owner, land survey agent, and speculator, proved also to be a scoundrel.)

**APRIL 1845** – Captain Barney presented a hydrographical map of the Upper Mississippi as completed by Nicola. This was the first mention made of a landing and harbor at lower end of Dubuque. Other landings and small harbors abounded at 4th, 7th, and 16th streets.

**NOVEMBER 1846** – Addressed to Captain Barney by the clerk: "Whereas some two years since an appropriation of $7500 was made by Congress for improvement of Dubuque Harbor, and subsequently an additional $7000 for that purpose, little or nothing has been done." The clerk calls Captain Barney, the U.S. Agent, to furnish a statement of the amount already expended, the balance remaining, and time necessary to complete the Harbor." (Council seemed very exasperated.)

**MAY 1847** – Mayor was requested by city council to open correspondence with Secretary of War relating to the Harbor.

**SEPTEMBER 1847** – Mississippi Islands were purchased to assure we could adjust them to our benefit. Iowa Senators Crawford and Benton and Representative Michael O'Brien made this possible.

**JUNE 1848** – Communication finally received from Captain Barney about the Harbor. Council refused to appropriate $375 more for the harbor. (Council thoroughly fed up with outgoing money and little progress.)

**JULY 1848** – Petition from business man McDonald was received to pave the wharf at the foot of 4th.

**JULY 1850** – A committee including Mathias Hamm was appointed to survey the river from Lorimer's Furnace up the inner sloughs and Lake Peosta (now called Peosta Channel) across to Eagle Point, estimating the cubic yards required to be removed to make a channel not less than four feet deep and sixty feet wide, effecting a good deep channel along the entire line of wharves. Bountiful croplands had now made Dubuque self-sustaining. Anything we could ship out was to our profit. Manufacturing of furniture, leather goods, cigars, mops, brooms and other household goods increased.

**NOVEMBER 1851** – 315 Dubuquers voted to secure a $20,000 loan for dredging the channel. 14 were opposed.

**MARCH 1851** – 10% bonds were issued to the amount of $2000 receivable in payment of Harbor tax. City Attorney Samuels contracted with Abel Hawley to build a dredge boat for $10,000. Harbor bonds were sent to New York to be sold. Four installments were paid to Hawley on the dredge boat.

**1852** – George Burton asked permission to cut a canal through the island opposite 1st and 2nd Streets to intersect the channel through which steamboats were admitted to the river. Able Hawley was paid $500 to dredge the Harbor. A copy of the proposed Dubuque Harbor by Barney was purchased.

**MAY 1852** – All the wharf lying between 2nd and 5th Streets was appropriated to the use of steamboats, providing 4th and 5th also to be used for other purposes. Permanent rock bank at this public landing to which steamboats could be tied was begun. Businessmen Stout and McHenry paid for the harbor improvements.

**JUNE 1852** – City Council argued that Captain Barney's plan no longer applied to present use of the city units. Dredging to a seven-foot depth between the public landing and main river was recommended. Because Dubuque's Harbor Tax had only realized $11,337.13 in revenue, Congress was petitioned for another appropriation.

**JULY 1852** – Progress on public landing included steamboat wharf secured by docking pavement well below low water mark, paving south side of 4th to south side of 5th with stone at least 4 inches thick and 9 inches deep below low water mark.

**AUGUST 1852**—Businessman Adams applied for location of a yard on public landing in which to build boats. The Honorable George W. Jones telegraphed the good news that Congress passed the River and Harbor Bill, which listed a grant of $15,000 for the Dubuque Harbor, and $100,000 for the rapids at Rock Island, IL. (Robert E. Lee and the Corps of Engineers did those improvements at Rock Island.)

**SEPTEMBER 1852** – Hawley was paid for dredging inner slough. In shallow places it was only 5 feet deep. Bids let for stonewalling of public docksides. Excavation and removal of material to adjoining streets at 1¢ a cubic yard.

**JANUARY 1853** – Contractors for canal excavation threatened to abandon work unless payment increased. Tax increases were needed.

**MARCH 1853** – Permission was granted for a ferry boat landing anywhere between the south side of 1st and north side of 2nd Street, and the use of Hawley's dredge before Harbor operations commenced.

**May 1853** – City Council agreement was made that Hawley's dredging of the canal would not conflict with Barney's government plan of Harbor Improvement.

**1854** – A cut was made through outer island to the outer slough. The City of Dubuque sold to Dubuque and Pacific Rail Co. the island between inner and outer sloughs. Suggestions were made to build a bridge, and to fix the harbor on the outer island. Hawley's dredge was piling dirt and sand in the way of the harbor improvement. Hawley was paid to move the dirt to extend 4th and 5th Streets rather than build a bridge or place flat boats on the slough there.

**SEPTEMBER 1854** – Breach of contract by Hawley and failure to complete dredging forced Dubuque to sue and achieve a settlement whereby Dubuque obtained the dredge boat for our own use. Filling of extensions of 6th, Dodge, and 7th through 11th Streets continued as canal deepening continued. A permanent bridge over the inner slough below Waples Cut and a bridge swinging 150 feet coming over the main slough were proposed. Permanent bridges were agreed upon above Barney Cut and below Waples Cut.

**1855** – Importance of Dubuque's lead had increased during the civil war efforts. Banker J. K. Graves owned the Shot Tower but conceived the idea of abandoning building such expensive towers in favor of using old mine shafts to drop lead. He'd been appointed Colonel at Camp Franklin in Dubuque with nearly 6,000 soldiers in camp. He later secured the Chicago, Dubuque, Clinton Railway which carried our freight south and west, and the Chicago, Dubuque, Minnesota Railway going north. River connection and shipping of lead at the river was busy.

**FEBRUARY 1855** – Land on the main shore was reserved by the city for public use. Stephen Hempstead, first practicing lawyer in Dubuque, after serving as Iowa Governor returned to Dubuque. He spent the rest of his life working to erect and improve Dubuque facilities.

**JUNE 1855** – Jones Street Harbor Company extended 1st Street to the main river and constructed and paved an 800-foot levee. The Illinois Central Railroad reached Dunleith, E. Dub., but failed to cross the river, so the Dubuque and Sioux City Railroad was formed by General Booth to go West.

**AUGUST 1855** – 7th St. Harbor Improvement said that if the city were to donate to Dubuque and Pacific Railway the upper half of the outer middle island for a freight depot, they would extend 5th across the slough to there.

**JANUARY 1858** – Dubuque requested the government to cease funding the digging out sloughs as this was interfering with our plans for a main harbor not located on the outer island but at our permanent wharves. Council asked funds solely for main habor.

**MARCH 1860** – Iowa Congress granted to Dubuque title to

all the sloughs and islands nearby to be improved as we saw fit, to fill up sloughs and low lying lands between Dubuque and the main river channel.

**SEPTEMBER 1864** – First mention of the Dubuque Ice Harbor to be developed by building wing dams to force water into the narrowest, deepest channel and getting rid of the sandbars, thereby providing a safe harbor for boats to lay up in winter and secure them from the breaking up of ice in the spring. The Ice Harbor would also provide a lucrative business for the repair and fitting out of boats for the Packet Company, and a convenient place for building barges.

**1865** – Dubuque and Dunleith Railroad Bridge, a 1,760-foot span made entirely of stone and iron, cost $750,000.

**MAY 1868** – Mayor authorized our Representative Allison to contact whoever had authority of the U. S. Congress to make surveys and remove obstructions to the navigation of the Upper Mississippi, inviting them to make a survey of our harbor and remove such obstructions as might fall within his jurisdiction and government appropriations.

**AUGUST 1868** – Major General Warren replied he would do all within his power as soon as the appropriations bill for Survey of North Western and Western Rivers was passed.

**1870** – *Dubuque Telegraph* printed that we had a population of 25,000, with a total of 41,000 county residents; the state of Iowa's population had reached one million. 40 men, many of them skilled wood carvers from Germany and Switzerland, were employed in furniture manufacturing. 50,000,000 feet of pine lumber from Minnesota and Wisconsin were sold through 15 Dubuque lumber yards. Barge traffic at the harbor increased.

**APRIL 1871** – Argument that "14 years of improvements are being washed away with every rise in the river, bridges rotted down, breaks in levees, all causing growth of an obstructive sandbar in front of the city. This must be removed. Try opening the canal from Lake Peosta down to the bridge on Washington and 7th, thence along the levee down to 1st where is the best and safest harbor on the Mississippi together with facilities for building and repairing boats and laying safely up in winter. Since places there have 12-foot depth at ordinary times, large tonnage ships can accommodate our industries."

**1875** – *Dubuque Telegraph* printed that shipments from Dubuque to southern markets included millions of barrels of flour, and bushels of wheat, barley, oats, and corn as well as live and dressed hogs. We now had 18 wagon and carriage shops selling 5,000 vehicles per year. We shipped in every direction all articles needed in agriculture, household economy, and most industries. Manufacturing included steam engines, boilers, threshing machines, castings, iron foundries, machine shops, copper works, furniture, woolens, flour, vinegar, produce, bricks, stone and sand, meat packing, metal stamping, and tin ware.

**SEPTEMBER 1882** – Army Corps of Engineers, Major Dunham, visited to confer on location of Ice Harbor: North side of 3rd St. Extension to a point 200 feet from its beginning, then South at right angles 164 feet, then East parallel with and distant from South side of 3rd St. 100 feet to levee on main Mississippi channel, said property to be used in perpetuity as an Ice Harbor. At least 50 feet of Booth and Stout properties on south side would be appropriated for a public levee and on the North boundary of the Harbor. Booth and Stout both wanted tradeoff of property by the city.

**OCTOBER 1882** – Moore and Linehan were hired by government to move 80,000 yards of material out of the harbor area before June 30. Debated using it to lay out two streets for Booth and Stout in consideration of their property being used. Council moved U. S. government to be authorized to dredge, improve, and maintain the Ice Harbor in perpetuity, the city reserving all municipal control and police regulation over the premises.

**JULY 1884** – Appropriation by U. S. River and Harbor Act for completion of Ice Harbor at Dubuque.

**MAY 1885** – North boundary to be a line 200 feet south of and parallel with South side of 3rd St. Ext., a strip 100 feet wide being reserved on North side of said Ice Harbor for a levee along entire north front of same. South boundary to be a line 110 feet North of and parallel with South side of 1st St., to be reserved and used as a levee. Levees approved on West side also.

**JULY 1886** – Lumber boats, rafts, and inhabited flat boats prohibited in Ice Harbor to make way for shipping only.

**JUNE 1889** – Harbor Master instructed to remove all houses, sunken crafts, and boats in Ice Harbor.

**AUGUST 1897** – Government dredging away sandbar at mouth of Ice Harbor created 75,000 yards of fill for land.

**SEPTEMBER 1899** – Senator Allison and Congressman Henderson reported $4,503.99 unexpended balance from Ice Harbor appropriation after successful completion with money available for maintenance. All the years of haggling meant Dubuque wound up with not only the Dubuque Ice Harbor, but also harbors at 4th, 16th and Shiras Avenue, to suit everyone's interests. A Coast Guard Station and landing and the Army Corps of Engineers operate from the south side of the Harbor, as does Newt Marina. Molo Sand and Gravel was on the Northeast corner. Dubuque Boat and Boiler Works was on the north side. Iowa Oil Co. and the old Diamond Jo Office were at the southeast corner with a public landing and launching site. True to tradition, Dubuquers sought and fought for government aid to ensure a safe flood wall after the devastating flood of 1965.

Always the Ice Harbor has meant Safe Harbor in Dubuque.

# Oil Rush – 1860

YOUNG HERMAN BRUSHED the last stroke of paint over his pasteboard stencil and peeled it back. The *J.G.* gleamed wet and black against the red barrel. Half of the row of initialed barrels had already dried in the smothering Pennsylvania sun on the boardwalk in front of Mr. Kellerman's store on Liberty Street in Pittsburgh.

"So, Herman," Mr. Kellerman's screw-eyes bored at him from the doorway, "You vant all der vorld should know to Johann Gottlob dese twenty-five barrels belong, no?"

"It was just something to do, sir, while Papa's gone to get a team and wagon." Herman spoke as correctly as any of the grammar school children in Ward Three. Two years is enough for any twelve-year-old to learn a spoken language. Mr. Kellerman was too old to manage any more than broken English. Papa was too stubborn.

"Your lettering, she is goot, Herman!" Hands forever jingling coins in his pockets, Mr. Kellerman sized up his shiny new plate glass window. "Mit der left ofer paint you could put up mine name yet inside der glass, maybe? *Abraham Kellerman Dry Goots.* Like a goot boy?" and he nudged Herman inside the store.

Herman studiously bent his tousled head to reverse the lettering on a scrap of paper so that it would read correctly from outside. With long, easy strokes he began to outline the name and fill
it in. Through the bubble-specked glass the store owner watched
in an agony of apprehension lest Herman drip or streak the paint.
Folks stopped to watch. Soon a crowd gathered admiring the
name and asking about the new barrels. Mr. Kellerman's squinty
eyes undid a notch or two, his fingers all the while dancing in
increasing delight among his silver pieces.

"Herman here a smart boy is, und also is his papa Johann
Gottlob. Efen now he vent to get der team mit vagon for hauling
der oil barrels. See how Herman painted der bottoms for stopping yet der leaks?"

"Oil!" "Indian medicine!" Crazy talk!" Amid hoots and
shouts, half the crowd took off, but a curious circle hung around
as Kellerman led Herman out and handed down from his shelf
a bottle of *SENECA OIL*. "Show dem same vey like your Papa
after supper last night at der boarding house."

With excitement pounding in his ears and embarrassment
fluttering his hands, Herman spilled the oil out upon the street
and gingerly struck a match to one edge. Yellow flames leaped
up and gulped away at the puddle, flickering smoke-edged blue,
and burning the ground black beneath. "You see," said Herman,
"Papa read in the Pittsburgh Gazette how they bored a well for
salt down the Ohio River near Smith's Ferry and struck instead a
light reddish oil they can burn in lamps without refining. He read
they were pumping six or eight barrels a day."

"My *SENECA OIL* yet!" Mr. Kellerman pointed out his own
label on his bottle: *For Healing Cuts and Bruises, for Injuries to*

*Horses Feet, and Stiff Joints or Rheumatism for Man or Beast.* "Since first I set up store haf der Seneca Indians gathered up dis oil off der creek mit blankets. Den dey wrung dem out into jars still und I buy it und sell it for my medicine. Now vat I do mit whole barrels full? Not so many sick horses in all Pennsylvania is."

"Put your hand over the fire!" cried Herman eagerly. Several men bent down to feel of the dwindling flames. "Papa says it will keep you warmer than coal and burn brighter than any lamp."

"Say, and the smell's not so bad as I heard tell," grinned Hans Schultz. "Johann has an idea to trade oil for gold, eh Kellerman?"

Wheeling to the sound of clattering wagon and gallumping horses, they watched Johann's dray sweep the corner wide and come to a dust-spitting stop. Johann leapt down and circled among them windmill fashion, flapping out his exciting news in jumbled German. He stopped, short of breath, clapping a hand on his son's shoulder. "Say dem how she is, boy." He slapped his broad-brimmed hat against his knee, swabbing the sweat from his face.

"We won't have to go way down the Ohio for oil after all. Papa says they just struck oil on the Allegheny River right here near Franklin, so he drove out in his new wagon and leased a place on Plummer Farm just a mile north of them. They look like big paying wells as soon as the pumping gets started. We'll have a well of our own in no time."

Johann interrupted, "Mit der horses und vagon, barrels, und lease, goes mine vages all. Yet some monies for der vell am I needing to get started."

All the men were sparked by Johann's fire. Mr. Kellerman, eyes now wide open, magically unpocketed clean paper and pen.

He proceeded to organize a little stock company, collecting all ready cash. They adjourned to his back room to complete plans.

Johann decided to return to the job he had just quit at the Pittsburgh Iron Works long enough to help design and forge necessary tools; chisel-shaped three-inch drills, reamers for rounding out the drilled holes, a shear made like two long links to jar the drills loose when they wedged tight in the rock, sand pumps for getting out the fine-chiseled rock, and grappling hooks. With the company's money he bought an eight horsepower oscillating cylinder steam engine and seven hundred feet of three-inch manila rope. All supplies were speedily shipped to the Plummer Farm.

Sharp and clear rang the axes those first days as Johann, Herman, and one hired hand hewed lumber to throw up an engine house and a four-bunk sleeping shanty. Cook and bunk house duties fell to Herman. To erect the derrick of four forty-foot-high posts was a job for men and horses. Herman was sure he'd pitched mountains of food and hay into hungry mouths, and poured rivers of water on over-heated backs and tempers before the engine was at last in place and the pulley atop the derrick ready for tools and rope. Then came interminable cords of wood to be chopped for the puffing engine that kept the drills chinking away at the well.

Suddenly one night the three awoke in their lonely little bunk-house to strange rushings and clatterings from the road just over the hill. They tumbled outside and stopped short.

"The heavens are on fire!" cried Herman.

"No, no. More like der Aurora Borealis she iss. See how she flashes now lighter, now darker?" Half the night sky to the north of them was a vivid pulsing red. Commotion up at the dark road drew them forward.

"Have you heard about the big fire at Oil Creek?" cried out the first man they ran into. "One of the owners of the big flowing well they just struck on the Buchanan farm lit a match to smoke a cigar. He was quite a distance from the flowing oil well but the air must have been full of the fumes. It went off like lightning and gunpowder! Everyone close was burned to death with the first breath of it. Plenty others up there hurt bad trying to save 'em or get their own belongings out safe. You must have heard the riders on horseback going to fetch doctors up from Franklin. Here comes one now!"

Out of the dark came the buggy, which stopped in haste to pick them up, then dashed on toward the glowing horizon. The doctor, no more dressed than they, asked for the full story as they rode. When they topped the hill overlooking the scene, the blazing fury of the whole flat and surrounding hills was partially hidden by a choking dense smoke. Struggling victims headed toward the buggy. The doctor was afraid to drop his frantic horse's reins, so they got down and loaded as many of the injured as possible into the buggy, heading the horse back toward Franklin for him.

Little or nothing could be done to stop the fire for several days until it had nearly burned out. Then, by shoveling into the well the earth which had itself been burned two or three feet deep, the fire was finally squelched. No amount of clearing out and pumping water on it could revive the well; it had been a funeral pyre for forty-four.

When the air had cleared, Johann calculated risk against possibility and went back to his own well operation in more determined haste than before. From blink of dawn to wink of stars they drilled. At length, down past several veins of water, at five hundred and four feet, a dark blue-green slime rose to the surface. Next came the task of forcing down below the lowest water vein heavy iron tubing with a leather seed bag at its end. This was filled with linseed to exclude the water so pure oil might rise. There was not enough gas in this pocket to force the oil out in a gusher. When pumping began, four or five barrels a day was the most they could raise.

Empire or Bennet Well and several other large flowing wells had by this time been struck. Derricks were springing up everywhere over night. Men swarmed to the oil fields. The Empire Well spewed out an estimated twenty-five hundred barrels of oil a day for a long time but they could not get materials to build tanks fast enough to contain it, so most of it flowed away into the creek and soaked the ground a great distance. Nobody was prepared for the enormous output of these first flowing wells. It went to waste.

"Herman, my boy," shouted Johann, "Vy do ve stay und sweat offer dis puddle ven dey haff oil und ve haff barrels?"

"And Mr. Kellerman could buy up more barrels for us if we'd want them," Herman sang back with perfect understanding. They turned their backs upon their well and set out to a new future as the first oil speculators.

Selling out the machinery and property to good advantage, they bought a supply of five hundred barrels and several wagon teams. They headed back up Oil Creek to the wells. Buying up large quantities of oil, they hauled it down road to the mouth of the creek which flowed into the Allegheny. Here they shipped the barrels on the steamboat *Allegheny Belle* to Pittsburgh where oil could be sold at a profit. Then buying any more barrels Kellerman might have cornered for them, they returned to repeat the venture. The red-ended barrels with the black *J.G.* and an added star were soon a familiar sight on riverboats. Others followed Johann's lead. The price of oil soon dropped to fifteen cents at the wells, while barrels cost three dollars and fifty cents empty.

Oil City reared up overnight at the mouth of the creek, a new frame structure going up every day. All roads from wells to city were soon axle-deep in oily mud as the wagons hauled their dripping cargo. Men, women, and boys alike had to wear hip-boots everywhere. On Sundays Herman's pockets bulged with silver coins after cleaning boots at the boarding house in Oil City.

Overflowing wells now made barrels out of the question, so oil buyers built sixteen-foot-square boxes three feet deep, partly covered with one-inch boards. Oil was piped into them at the wells, measured and paid for. But getting them down creek to the steamers was a new problem.

One day a seedy little gent with a shoestring tie circulated among oil buyers. "Got a sawmill upcreek twenty miles or so from Oil City. Built dams to save water for a pond freshet. Makes an artificial high-water rise of about five feet when the dams are opened. Changes the creek to a good-flowing stream for about two hours. Good transportation! Cheap! Could open the dams every Friday noon. Charge $2 for any oil raft that uses the freshet."

"That's not cheap!" complained the oilmen.

"Your predicament. My answer," was his only reply.

Falling in with his suggestion, they built rafts. Oil boxes were loaded on during the week to shoot down on the freshet each

Friday. Because the creek was flooded so much higher than the low river stage, riding the rapids quickly became a popular but risky business. Several hundred rafts would be loaded and eager to get to the river before the freshet was spent. They cut loose as thick as the creek could carry them. Some, having set out six or eight miles down to be ahead of a hundred others, would get so far ahead of the rise they would ground on sandbars or rocks until the oncoming water pushed them free to float.

"Three hundred fifty barrels und all snug!" Johann shouted to his son one placid Friday.

"Let's go, then. It's ten to noon," Herman called back from the slippery bank. He yanked the slipknot loose and leapt to his father' side aboard the raft. Together they poled out, third in line on the sluggish creek. Others were cutting loose in quick succession behind them. All toiled rapidly along, tensely steadied for the rush of water which would sweep down from behind, catapulting them headlong round the bend and under the bridge to Oil City.

"Ve're getting too far ahead. Ve'll ground, sure!" Johann called back anxiously as they maneuvered the bend.

"Look out for the bridge pier!" cried Herman.

Johann gave a hard shove with an oar against the stone pier. They slid safely under the bridge only to jolt solidly onto the bank below. Two rafts ahead were safely under way, but the one just behind them grounded before reaching the bridge. Her oarsmen tried desperately to straighten her as the rumble of oncoming water was heard. The first rise of water swept the raft square against the pier in midstream. Boxes were flung high up on the pier, spilling their oil into the creek, oars flying, knocking the men down into the oily mess. The momentum swung the boat end round and closed up the channel under one half of the bridge.

Another boat next struck this amidships and swung round, closing up the other side of the channel, blockading the entire creek with several hundred oil boats sweeping round the bend unaware of any danger. As their oars struck the blockade, each raft swung about with lightning rapidity, throwing men into the rushing water, oil, and wrecked boats, crushing, drowning, killing them. Wreckage sank back filling with water. Such a formidable dam was piled across the creek that the following boats were hoisted high into the air as they crashed, spilling all their cargo into the creek.

"Look out! Stop! Danger ahead!" Their throats went dry as their warnings were drowned in the thundering waters. Herman and Johann stood clutching the bridge railing above, where they and a handful of others uninjured had struggled to climb and watch in horror, hot and cold chills sweeping over them. They stood transfixed as the shocking catastrophe of smashing boats piled up before their eyes.

Silence followed the crashing of the last barge. They shook themselves into action. Stumbling down the bank, they searched for survivors and pulled onto shore the dead bodies. Oil ran several feet thick down creek as the freshet was spent. A million dollars worth of oil floated down the Allegheny that night.

"Maybe is now our turn to pull out vhile ve can, und buy der farm nice und safe, eh, son?" Johann flung a loving arm round his frightened son.

"That farm can wait but this oil won't. Let's stick it out if we can," Herman said, straightening his shoulders.

"As stubborn a German as effer your Papa! Ve'll help clear der wreckage. Den tomorrow ve haff our own boat pulled off der bank und back to verk!"

Giant gushers of oil wait not for fire or death. More men undaunted came to tackle this colossus. Once again the creek became a rollicking oil traffic lane. Warehouses were built in Oil City to store the surplus. Supply now outgrew both market and transportation.

One inky night the pilot of a large oil raft set out from the docks at Oil City in a little skiff. Lantern held high, he peered anxiously forward to the sandbar at the mouth of the creek. His raft had stuck there in mid-afternoon and sprung a leak. Fading daylight was wasted trying to budge her loose. Now he hoped to locate the leak and at least repair her before daylight. There'd be no danger as the boat was entirely boarded over.

Flickering lantern rays barely made her visible when— KABOOM! The entire boat exploded. A sheet of orange flame wreathed in black clouds jettisoned skyward. The atmosphere quaked. People back in Oil City felt the explosion's vacuum pull against their eardrums as much as hearing the actual sound. Neon blazing sky was visible all the way to the next county.

Fire spread to Oil City, engulfing the entire town. Her frame buildings and warehouses popped like kegs of gunpowder. Herman and Johann fled with the townspeople to the hills. Watching the raging inferno, Johann whispered, "Here, take care off dis. No vone vill expect to find it on you." He slipped his leather pouch containing $4000 in paper money under Herman's shirt. Then he called out, "I'm going back down dere to see iff I can help anyone out. How about some uff you udder men?" They shouldered out from among the women and children to march into battle against this unleashed monster.

Herman manfully tightened his belt and buttoned his jacket close, burning with pride at being entrusted with all his father's savings. The responsibility lasted longer than he'd hoped. Not until all the oil stocks in town were devoured was the fire mastered.

Oil flow continued, and adventure as well. While Johann and Herman had good luck amid these mishaps, they sweated and bled for their $4000. One there was, a penniless tramp, who came upon the scene now. In talking with a Mr. Phillips at the boarding house, he discovered Phillips had taken a lease on the Tar Farm and had an engine but no money to continue boring operations. The tramp offered to be partner, do half the work for half the profits. After all, he had nothing to lose. The Phillips Well struck a gusher and turned out seven hundred fifty barrels a day, making them rich men.

"Too cheap," objected Phillips when oil prices dropped below fifteen cents a barrel. "I will not sell at such a price, nor do I propose to have any more oil flow into the ground and creek!" He put a stopcock on his well, turning off the flow. "Now, when oil gets to a decent price, we'll let her run." About twenty other well owners followed suit.

"In the name of all things Confederate! What's going on here?" roared Phillips one day when he opened his stopcock to refill his own oil tank. Nothing came out! "She must be clogged," he stammered. "We'll try pumping her out. If need be, we'll take out the chambers, ream her out, sand pump her clean, and put down new tubing." Still no oil. Someone else had struck the same vein in a better place and was getting all the flow. Nothing remained for Mr. Phillips and partner but a little gas.

"The Phillips Well's gone dry!" spread down the line. All other well stopcocks were opened allowing oil its natural flow, reaping profit as long as oil lasted.

Young Herman leaped from the raft to creek bank at Oil City one mint-crisp morning and made fast. He settled into the mud the gangplank Johann thrust toward him. Straightening up, Herman's ears caught a weird rustling above the slapping sound of the waters. He glanced out over the Allegheny, then dashed aboard calling, "Papa, there's an army marching south to the river!"

"Gray or Blue?" Johann shouted back, swinging round, letting the first oil barrel slip from his grasp and clatter down the gangplank.

"Gray, and Red, and Black, too," laughed Herman pointing.

"Squirrels yet!" Johann gazed in astonishment. "Dere must be tousands of dem."

"They certainly are marching like they know where they're going. The river's not going to stop them, either." Herman scratched his tousled hair in wonder. With determination and dispatch of generals leading their army, they headed to the bank of the wide shallow river and plunged in. Swimming straight across, they were followed in close rank by the entire body of squirrels. The width of the stream was churned frothy, dotted with their slick bobbing little heads. Many arrived on the opposite shore looking like drowned rats, too exhausted to go on. Some little boys came running to pick them up or knock them with sticks until they had as many as they wanted to carry home.

However, the main body of squirrels shook their bedraggled fur and marched off toward the big woods near the Clarion River, disappearing as fast as they had appeared.

"Why do you suppose they're moving south?" Herman pondered the slimy polluted creek water. "All this oil and the gas smell?"

"Or could be dey think all dese fires on der hillside iss making dere food scarce," commented Papa Johann setting to his task unloading barrels.

Johann and Herman found such a tie-up of oil supplies at Oil City they talked with several raft owners about relieving the congestion. By lashing five or six individual rafts together at the creek mouth, and using all hands, they could easily guide the one large barge down the Allegheny to Pittsburgh.

"Vonce ve learn der low vater channel," prophesied Johann, "Ve'll haff no troubles." But he reckoned without Rattlesnake Falls, Patterson Falls, five bridges and some large sandbars. For every successful trip there was a troublesome one.

"All hands out!" when they were stuck caused all to jump into the water to build wing dams of the largest boulders they could find, thus converting the channel into a narrower, deeper lane. Taking poles and handspikes, they would push the barges over the spot into deeper water.

"It's getting worse by the week. If fall rains don't set in soon, we'll be stranded here for sure," Herman complained, and they were, for the remainder of the summer, stuck at the mouth of the Clarion by a lonely pine forest.

"Vat haff ve here, son?" Johann pointed out the little orange-red bonfires floating eerily downriver toward them. Fishermen were copying a primitive Indian fishing art. They drifted at night in flat-bottomed boats with iron framework suspended over the stern just above water line. In these iron baskets they burned pine splints and pitch pine knots, the fire enabling them to spot fish six or eight feet below on the riverbed. It's quite a trick for a spear-man to aim, allow for refraction of vision at the water line, and still strike a fish just back of the head. They thrust down, pulling up large pike, pickerel, or bass. Tossing them into the flat boats, they aimed again as they floated on.

"Keep avay! Move off!" shouted the Gottlobs as the fire bas-kets drew dangerously near their oil. "Anyvay ve vork it ve lose," sighed Johann. "Should ve stand guard und lose time still, or go back for anuder raft und haff dis raft burn up?" They camped overnight, standing guard till rain finally launched them.

Rain belied them as well. One raft load made it safely to Sharpsburg, five miles above Pittsburgh, and tied up for the night. Too much high water and carroming driftwood broke the raft loose in the night. Next day father and son set out in a skiff but had to go past Allegheny City and a great way down the Ohio before finding a few empty boxes stranded here and there along the shore. Raft and cargo had been demolished.

"Pipelines! That's what's needed here!" A farsighted young man named Rockefeller, who'd started as an office boy at four dollars and fifty cents a week, brought to the oil fields the solu-tion to their impossible situation. He sold the well owners on his new idea.

"If you will all cooperate in laying pipelines from your wells to Oil City, I can guarantee safe, cheap delivery. This is too big a thing for barrel shipping. All we need is a little organization.

There are large moneyed interests in New York I can persuade to invest in the enterprise. The third step will be to invite the oil refineries to unite with our company. We must build a railroad into Oil City. If we had big steel tanks built right on the flatcars, it would simplify matters all around. I tell you, once we try it, railroads all over the United States and even Canada will want to carry our tankers. You're letting your fortune slip through your fingers. If you join the company, I'll build you a network to a nationwide market. Oil will come into her own!"

"No, my son," Johann gazed across the river to the hills. "Four years ve verk here. Iss now der time to count up our profit und buy dat timber farm. Ve haff enough money to send back to der old country und bring Mama und der girls offer. Und money to see us trough der first year or two. Iss more dan I dreamed."

"But Papa, why should Rockefeller be the one to get so rich?"

"On vat you put in iss vat you get out, no?" Johann wagged a patient head at the boy. "Ve brought four-hundred dollars in savings, und der best ideas ve had. Rockefeller brought der answer yet!"

"I guess he can't eat any more meals, or enjoy them any more than the rest of us," agreed Herman.

"America, she's been goot to us, no?"

"Yes, Papa!"

They turned from the oil fields and walked on, arm in arm.

# Look Out for Spies

SECURITY AT DUBUQUE during World War II was mostly centered on anti-German and anti-Japanese sentiments. Emotions ran high. Germans in Dubuque wished they could fade into the woodwork. Those who sent care packages to beleaguered relatives surreptitiously hid the addresses of underground contacts from nosey people standing in line at the Post Office. Germans modified their very names to blend into the population. They bought War Bonds and went to extremes to show their patriotism.

On May 29, 2003, in Irvine, California, the death of Dubuque's retired longtime Lockmaster, Arturo Ayala, brought to mind the incident when he met up with Dr. Hertz, professor at the University of Dubuque, back in 1942. Mr. Ayala, a swarthy Latino, had not only the safety of Lock and Dam #11, the Iowa Wisconsin Bridge, and the Mississippi River in his care, but also his family. His pretty, petite wife, Evelyn, and their two young daughters were living in the neat white Lockmaster's house adjacent the locks.

Early one morning Mr. Ayala noted the tall erect silhouette against the skyline directly above him at Eagle Point Park viewing station. The man spent an hour taking pictures and watching the barges lock through. When this same figure later appeared down at lockside still taking snapshots, Mr. Ayala phoned the local FBI Office to report the blond military-looking man wearing a felt hat with a feather cockade in it. Within the hour Dr. Hertz was apprehended for questioning, his camera confiscated, and the film destroyed.

Actually Dr. and Mrs. Hertz were political refugees from Germany hired by the University to teach here. Coming from Germany where, for centuries, the entire length of the Rhine River banks had been riprapped to control floods, Dr. Hertz was in awe of the beauty and breadth of the unconfined shorelines of the Mississippi at Dubuque. Had he been an artist, he would have painted the powerful panorama, but he was a writer of political philosophy so he took photos instead. Needless to say the FBI ripped out his film and thoroughly investigated his motives and background. Unlike most hapless refugees, he had the University to come to his defense and vouch for his behavior throughout the war.

What a furor of gossip and innuendo snaked across the university campus. However, Dr. Hertz and his wife were already a favorite couple who provided dignity plus glamour at events. When they chaperoned dances, the entire dance floor cleared at any waltz tune to watch with rapt attention while Dr. Hertz swirled his lovely lady in sweeping spirals around the room.

Mrs. Hertz always wore at these affairs a slender white gown with a bottom flounce that fanned out like a circle of flower petals. She was blonde, blue-eyed, healthy-cheeked, and wore her hair in a soft wave from forehead to just below the ear. The coeds' fancy, curly hairstyles then in fashion required tight curlers and pin-curls overnight. After seeing her, most of the girls started copying her gentler hairstyle. She was a shy sorority sponsor.

The stunning Hertz couple were reserved, but once at the second floor rotunda railing of Steffens Hall looking down upon the Homecoming Queen who was gazing with adoration at her football captain, Dr. Hertz was heard to say with an aging man's sigh, "One could wish to be a football captain."

Though this foreigner was no threat to our security, not a Nazi spy at all, he found our security threatening to him, and our scoundrels as well. Upon completing a book for publication, Dr Hertz innocently allowed a wily student from the Bronx to hand deliver the manuscript to the New York publisher during Christmas vacation rather than trust the mail.

Months went by without word from the publisher. Dr. Hertz finally phoned and the publisher investigated, only to discover the student had removed title and author pages, replacing them with his own. It was straightened out, and the culprit punished. It showed that, not just foreigners but nationals, too, can be a threat to society.

# Class of '42

RED, WHITE (HAIR, that is), and Blue Senior High colors abounded at the sixtieth class reunion of the class of 1942. Bill Martin skimmed in on his walker. Evelyn Matz and Bill Patton leaned on canes. What a great class! Those attending the game were glad to be asked to stand and be recognized because the bleacher seats at the football game had been so cold.

Of 335 members, 311 had graduated and 116 were still around to attend this reunion. At the banquet tributes were paid to the dead, and especially to those who had enlisted during World War II and died before graduation time—Jim Carney, Chuck Doran, and Don Dolphin. Some of those remembered had gone straight from welding class out to California's coastal ship-building and airplane factories. At every table the men who had served in the Army, Navy, Army Air Corps, and Marines were regaling one another with their tales of war. Bob Richards was supposed to be in Texas that week for a reunion with his sailor buddies from the destroyer *Claxton*, but chose to come home to Dubuque instead. All the wives remarked upon the camaraderie warming the banquet room at the Hoffman House.

"My classmates didn't even know one another," said Lanette from South Bend, Indiana.

"There were thousands in our New York senior class. We only got to know a few and never had reunions," said June.

Master of Ceremonies Ruth Mackert Rettenmaier and Gene Rettenmaier outdid their recurring performances with jokes and patter as they called classmates up to speak. Gene told the one about the Priest complaining about lesser accommodations in Heaven than the paint storeowner had.

"But this is the first paint store owner who ever made it to Heaven," explained St. Peter, and they brought the local paint baron Bob Sullivan to speak. Always the hub of the reunions, Sully described the gentler side of our Principal Bulldog Johnson, who once politely asked him, "Since you always come to school a half hour tardy every day, should I start school a half hour later every day to suit you?" He also gave Bob boxing gloves and offered to fight things out with him.

While Sully was the hub, Lorraine Heer Humke, the lady in red, has always been the glue, finding classmates and making arrangements stick. The twelve-member committee arranged a pre-game chili supper at Summit U.C.C. and a Hospitality Room with memorabilia, a Friday Banquet and Sunday Brunch at the Hoffman House, plus a Saturday boat ride on the *Spirit of Dubuque*. Fashion plate of the event was Betty Knight Krieg in a wild print silk dress with perfectly matched brilliant linen jacket, purse and shoes.

Jim Lenehan reminisced about old Dubuque theaters lining Main Street starting with the Strand on 12th (the easiest to sneak into through the side door), the *State* on Tenth (the most modern), the *Avon* on Ninth (which sold gummy bits, popcorn, licorice nibs, and sodas), the *Palace* (a stinky little hole in the wall with no ventilation where you could watch Tom Mix Saturday mornings for a nickel), and the quality theaters *Grand* and *Orpheum* (third balcony nickel seats) where many famous performers appeared. Out on Twenty-Second and Central was the *Capitol* (for a dime you could stay all day for continuous showings), and the dinky little *Varsity* up on Loras next to Rettenmaier Flooring close to the college crowd. Jim must have spent his high school years at the movies.

John Diehl and Jim Paisley told of working for Howard Hughes in the airline industry. "I worked for him four years and never saw the man," commented Paisley. Bob Patton came out of the Airborne Parachute Troops and used his expertise to become a smoke jumper for the Forest Service.

Betty Wharton and niece accompanied husband Don to the Mayo Clinic for esophageal surgery. When asked who those beautiful blondes were, Don said, "They're both mine."

"Way to go! More power to you," shouted a ninety-year-old woman in the waiting room. Don recalled eating the dry Army rations in Germany, particularly the dehydrated potatoes, with only snow to moisten them, so dry rations were *really dry*.

Don Breitbach conducted a statistical survey. "How many had a crush in grade school?" A show of hands. "A Junior High crush?" A show of hands. "How many married their High School sweetheart?" Many hands went up. "How many are still married to that sweetheart?" Very few hands went down. "How many dated Fred Thomas?" Hands up all over the room. So Fred must have dated the cheerleading squad, and all the Girls Athletic Assiciation before Dorothy Hennings corralled him. Dorothy sang a song with her high sweet voice but no microphone. She was drowned out by the vibrant keyboard accompaniment.

Bob Richards described Tennis for Seniors as missing the ball because you couldn't see it coming, or you couldn't see it going by, or you weren't ready, or you ducked and called out "FORE!" thinking this was golf, or you ran up to the net, grabbed the ball, wrestled it to the ground hugging it beneath your chest and shouted "Touchdown!" and lay there playing dead until the ball boys cleared the court, loading you into a cart and giving you a free ride back to the clubhouse. (He must have known whereof he spoke, because he one month later died of a heart attack.)

Dr. Merril Vanderloo choked at dinner and, amid flashing ambulance lights, was rushed to Finley Emergency Room. Within ten minutes word came back that a piece of chicken bone had been successfully removed from his throat and all was well. Dr. Charles Landgraf gave a dim opinion of HMOs and Managed Care Plans because they were less interested in people than in patient counts and profits. "They're crazy! They should see a psychiatrist!" said this just-retired psychiatrist. "Too bad I retired."

Don Harris told of parachute jumping into Saipan, landing on a pistol he didn't even know was in his pack. John Owens said upon enlisting in the Marines, he was asked, "Can you type?" He could. At once they slapped Sergeant stripes on him and sent him to their Des Moines office to help relieve the enlistment turmoil. Once the pressure eased, he was bumped back to Private. He spent most of his service in the China Burma India Theater. Bob Richards, once aboard a destroyer, was tossed a gun and gunbelt and told he was the Quartermaster, though he'd never handled a gun. Remembrances of war permeated this class as no other and sadly dominated school recollections, but teachers were recalled with cheers.

From the poolside balcony our reunion photo, after many pleas to quit turning around, quit horsing around, quit talking, look up and smile, finally captured us behaving like adults in our shiny pates and snowy hairdos, half as many as ten years ago, but still radiating school spirit. Bob Patton said, "The unique experience of the Dubuque schools, teachers, coaches, and classmates is more valued than words can express." The only sour note of the weekend was that, while everybody else enjoyed the river ride, Jeanne Frohs Baldwin and Jim missed the boat because they couldn't find the dock. A twenty-fifth reunion in town that same weekend looked at us oldies bemusedly, but we all voted to hold a sixty-fifth reunion, and be back for even the seventieth.

# Come to the River

COME TO THE river! Come to the National Mississippi River Museum and Aquarium. Come to flotillas and celebrations. Why do people come to the river? Because the Mississippi's wide swath is magnetic, moving, majestic, mighty, magical? The very hills tumble down to caress its shores. Natives and the first settlers were drawn to it. Those of us who love it call ourselves "river rats." The Mississippi owns us.

Prairie du Chien, a riverside plain meaning "Dog's Prarie," was a favorite gathering place of the Sioux, Winnebago, Sac, Fox, Iowa, Chippewa, Menominee and Pottawatomies who recognized the Father of Waters as a neutral meeting ground for making treaties, for trading with early white settlers, and for socializing. A great Indian game of lacrosse with two teams of 500 on a side was once played before 4000 onlookers there.

Marquette and Joliet braved the confluence of the Wisconsin and Mississippi Rivers to get the first white man's glimpse of the Upper Mississippi in 1673. They supped on the Iowa side but retreated to their canoes for sleep.

Next came Father Hennepin from LaSalle's exploration party

paddling from the Illinois River up the Mississippi in 1680, only to be captured by the Sioux somewhere between Dubuque and Prairie du Chien areas and not rescued for three months. Hardly an auspicious beginning for this stretch of the Mississippi.

Five years later LaSalle ordered Nicholas Perrot to build a fort on the Wisconsin River where it joined the Mississippi, Fort St. Nicholas. It was used for storage of furs. Word of the rich lead and fur sources here spread all the way to Europe. By 1755 white families had started settling on the Wisconsin banks of the Mississippi, drawn by fishing and trading in furs and lead, and by limitless lumber and easy transportation. The Treaty of Versailles made this French area into English land. When the land west of the Mississippi was transferred to Spain in 1779, it is believed that the English burned down the fort.

Julien Dubuque canoed down the Wisconsin in 1783 to trade at what would become, within two years, the white settlement of Prairie du Chien. Julien paddled his canoe over to the Iowa side pursuing the rich sources of lead. Sometimes he swam, leading his horse over. He and his fellow Frenchmen befriended the Sac and Fox Indian bands, and made their homes on the Iowa banks of the Mississippi. Within three years Julien had drawn up a contract at Prairie du Chien with Chief Peosta and five Indian villages, securing for himself possession of the lead mines and use of the land "as far as the eye could see."

Transporting the lead down to St. Louis on the fast flowing Mississippi in canoe or on flatboat was easy. Poling produce back upriver was the hard part, but still easier than travel overland. So the Mississippi drew settlers by facilitating commerce.

Because the Indians jealously guarded their Iowa land and

mines, Dubuque was the only white settler, while Prairie du Chien in Wisconsin had grown to 65 by 1800.

The land was once more transferred to France and bought by Jefferson. After 1803 Lt. Zebulon Pike's Army Inspection column crossed the Mississippi to keep an eye on the newly purchased territory called Louisiana. All these land transfers gave Dubuque the appellation "The City of Five Flags."

Fort Shelby and later Fort Crawford were built on the Wisconsin side, strategic for Army oversight to keep settlers out of the new territory and peace among the Indians. By 1806 John Jacob Astor had established his fur trading post on the river. Lead and furs from the Mississippi area fed the Army's growing needs, and the growing demands of the eastern seaboard and even Europe. Indian Agent Henry Schoolcraft was tempted across the river in 1820 to explore and make notes about Indian lore and history.

River commerce was made easier with the arrival of the first steamboat, the *Virginia*, at Prairie du Chien in 1823. By 1828 the first trading steamboat, *Galena*, landed and loaded at Dubuque. Army outposts were training grounds for later notables like Zachary Taylor, Jefferson Davis, Henry Dodge, and Winfield Scott. Though Julien Dubuque had died and the Fox Indians had taken back their land, this spot on the Mississippi became a magnet for miners like the Langworthy brothers. They would sneak across in spite of the Army and mine lead, even hiding the extracted ore on islands until such times as an Indian treaty with the U.S. would make it legal to exploit. The miners took up where they had left off. The river opened monumental doorways of adventure and opportunity into the Iowa territory.

Medicine came to Iowa when Army Surgeon Dr. Beaumont

conducted experiments from 1829 to 1831 on Alexis St. Martin, who had a hole torn in his stomach wall by gunshot. These experiments form the basis of our knowledge about digestion. Alexis lived until 1880, although the doctor died in 1853.

Education came to the Iowa banks of the Mississippi when the government signed a treaty in 1832 for a Winnebago children's school with boarding, lodging, the "three Rs," and agriculture. To keep the children away from the bad influence of "firewater" and unscrupulous traders, a tract of land was picked on the Iowa side, showing liquor and licentiousness had already come to the river. Iowa Indians already had gambling and corn to their credit. For that Indian Mission School, farm oxen, cows, and horses were brought across the river from Illinois into Iowa.

Families came to Iowa. The family of Hosea Camp was the first full family to come and live in the Dubuque area. James and Ezekiel Lockwood started lumber rafting. Population boomed within a year. By 1833 both Catholic and Protestant religions had established themselves.

Romance came to the river here when the *White Swan* arrived in 1835. After a gay party and patriotic ball, Knoxie Taylor, daughter of Zachary, and Jefferson Davis left on the boat to Galena where they were married upon arrival. Earlier the first Dubuquers wed were Mr. McCabe and Miss Mary Finley.

Art came to the river when George Catlin visited here in 1837 and painted pictures of Indians which today hang in the National Gallery at Washington, D.C.

Dubuque became a magnet for farmers, lumbermen, businessmen, lawyers, politicians, shipbuilders and shopkeepers. The Mississippi pulled wave after wave of progress with it as canoe,

raft, and keel boat gave way to paddlewheel, barge, tugboat, steamboat, and screw propeller, through wood, coal, steam, gasoline,
and diesel engines. Dredges such as the William Black deepening
the channel and clearing it of trees, snags, sunken boats, rocks,
and other obstructions aided traffic. The Honorable George W.
Jones pushed Congress to pass the 1852 Rivers and Harbors Bill
authorizing $15,000 for Dubuque Harbor and $100,000 for clearing the rapids at Davenport. Robert E. Lee earned his experience
as a commander directing the U.S. Army Corps of Engineers
blasting rocks and clearing a safe channel through those rapids.
The Corps added marker buoys and made channel maps available to encourage safe barge line industry as well as private boating craft.

Prosperity brings pleasure and time to luxuriate. One could
get drunk with the pleasure of boating rocked in the arms of the
Mississippi. Pleasure boats and powerboats developed into both
industry and pastime. The first Upper Mississippi River Grand
Excursion of 1854 was led by President Millard Fillmore trav-
elling in the company of a flotilla of boats from Rock Island to
St. Paul, Minnesota, examining first-hand the results of all the
money Congress had spent improving transportation, thus bringing attention to America's River and the largely unknown western frontier.

Dubuque had its first *Flotilla in 1910* and *Regatta in 1911*
when members of the Dubuque Boat Club and the M.V.P.B.A.
cruised down the Mississippi to Alton, Illinois, and up the
Illinois River to Peoria led by Commodore St. Claire Ede in *his
Elater IV,* which boasted two three-cylinder Schepple engines
driving twin propellers, a raised pilothouse, a dining room

drop leaf table, buffet, and sliding berths, an after cabin with piano, rattan chairs, four bunks, a galley sink, a refrigerator, and a toilet. The Herrmann brothers followed in their launch, the *Rosalie,* which boasted only a waterproof canopy, a steering wheel, a two-cylinder two-cycle engine, and seating for eight on each side.

At Bellevue they picked up Mr. Huey's *Red Top,* a thirty-five-foot mahogany speedboat with reinforced bottom for an eight-cylinder, two-hundred-fifty-horsepower engine, and Mr. Kelso's *Comet,* a twenty-five-foot speedboat with a one-hundred-ten-horsepower engine, both of which set world speed records at the Peoria races. Negotiating the bridge and long sandbars at Lyon, stopping for lunch, fuel, and sparkplug cleaning at Clinton, the *Rosalie* was then tied alongside *Elater IV* for the rapids at LeClaire. A professional pilot was hired to take them through fifteen miles of rapids above Davenport. Passing Muscatine, Burlington, and Ft. Madison, the *Flotilla* caught up with Mr. Dixon's *Lad,* a stern paddlewheeler with a powerful one-cylinder diesel engine. He led the way through Keokuk canal and locks, skirting the rapids. As yet there was no large dam and power plant there.

They passed a large carnival at LaGrange, MO., and reached Quincy, IL., one of the *Diamond Joe Packet Line's* ports with its large freight houses. At Kampsville they hurried to make out papers listing name, tonnage, passengers, and to get through the locks. They saw at the levee a big floating theater, the *Colley-Thom,* anchored where its brilliant lights reflecting on the waters drew the entire population to the Mississippi River. Dr. Philpots who had pushed his houseboat, *Idle Hour,* seven-hundred-fifty miles from Ft. Madison and back with his own little launch, lashed onto the *Lad* through the locks.

Passing Mark Twain's Hannibal, Missouri, and entering the mouth of the Illinois at Grafton, slower sailing upriver spread the *Flotilla* out, but many more boats en route from St. Louis to Peoria joined in. After Beardstown, Havanna, and Quiver Beach, they arrived at Peoria where a huge crowd of boaters and onlookers met at the Boat Club Dock to enjoy the races on Lake Peoria. Mr. Ede and Mr. Collins put a banner on *Elater IV* advertising the next *Regatta of 1911* at Dubuque. The *Flotilla* returned over the Hennepin Canal, going through thirty-one locks. In some places the canal crossed ravines in cement troughs, finally coming out at Moline lock and canal.

Committees of the Dubuque Boat Club made plans and sent invitations up and down river for all to come to that 1911 Dubuque River Regatta and Flotilla. Grandstands were erected south of the harbor to watch a triangular course set from High Bridge to Rock Cut. Dubuque boaters hung out pennants and sailed up to Cassville to escort visiting boaters to the harbor. What turmoil from the boats and cheering crowds who looked on! The froth of hundreds of small craft speeding to and fro made this a high point of the boating season. Crowds came to celebrate the 150th anniversary of that 1854 President Fillmore Grand Excursion. Will they come for the 175th anniversary? Oh, yes. They'll come. The Mississippi owns us.

# Spanish-American War Correspondence 1899

Sgt. Leo Fischer, Company G, Infantry
Manila, Philippines, November 23,1899

Mr. Richard Herrmann, Dubuque, Iowa

Dear Uncle,

Christmas greetings if this arrives in time. Excuse me for addressing you this way, but having been in Omaha so long hearing the folks refer to you as Uncle Richard, it comes naturally to me. Knowing you take great interest in art and science, and being able to see and obtain things you've no chance to over in the States, I think an exchange of letters would interest us both. I sent you a few postcards and papers in Chinese and Kanaka from Honolulu. Am sending a little package with things I picked up in Angeles, my present residence, a little town sixty miles from Manila on the Daquipan R.R. It is wrapped in a Spanish flag and contains one letter in the native language, Pampango, and another in Chinese, a document about a cattle sale, a Spanish prayer book, a piece of music, and what I deem most valuable: an insurgent payroll and muster-roll counter-signed by General Luna, whom Aguinaldo had murdered. I captured the latter two documents along with the company records of Third Company, First Battalion of Riflemen in our advance on Malbalakal, I was first man to enter their headquarters building and nailed a wicked-looking knife, two bayonets, and these documents. An officer made me relinquish the arms to him as I was absent without leave and had gone with the regulars on my own hook. I didn't dare claim them. *

*My writing was interrupted . It was eight-thirty and I was writing this letter on my desk (a tomato box) when suddenly the Captain burst in and told me to issue a day's rations and go with the company. It was a surprise, but half an hour later all of us marched to the railroad where we loaded into boxcars. We rattled on through the night guessing at our destination and prospects of a good hard battle. We rode ten miles and left the train at Calulut. The outposts of Company C stationed there had been fired upon by the enemy. F and G Companies stationed at Angeles had been ordered to clean out the "gou-gous." We marched four or five hours through mud and sand, wading rivers, breaking through jungle, etc. It was a wonderful moonlit night. At the little village of Mexico, we captured seven horses and two men, but Aguinaldo's men had taken to their heels. We arrived at Calulut at two-thirty a.m. and slept until five on the damp plaza. In the morning we built fires and fried our bacon and cooked coffee in our tin cups. We then marched out of town, formed lines of skirmishers, and went through a rice field, but found no one. We boarded our boxcars for home. Forty of my company of eighty-six are now sick with fever. Cholera is rampant here. I'm feeling just as fit as ever. I resigned as quartermaster as I didn't like it. Now I am duty sergeant.

They are keeping me quite busy now as an interpreter. Besides my German and French, I know Spanish well from being in Mexico and South America. At present I am studying the Pampango language spoken by the natives here, writing a little dictionary of Pampango. Our litter-bearers are mostly Macabebes, our teamsters Chinese with water buffaloes and two-wheeled carts. The Macabebes are enemies of the Tagalos who are on the insurgents' side. They've been great help to us, and know no fear.

This place is being rapidly repopulated as all natives have been allowed to return. Let's hope the bandit, Aguinaldo, will soon be at our mercy. Dealing all day long with Spanish prisoners and natives, I will soon be well acquainted with affairs on the islands, which are really complicated. I hope we may be able to exchange our opinions. I remain with best regards to your family,

Most Sincerely,
Leo Fischer

*　　*　　*

Miss Rosalie Herrmann
2419 Couler Ave. Dubuque, Iowa

Dear Cousin Leo,

We wish you a Merry Christmas and a very Happy New Year. We sincerely hope the New Year will bring only good things and also that you will be out of harm's way and in good health. Is the war in the Philippines about over or just commencing? The papers state that some of our American soldiers were sent to China. The Boer War played out after a while. Maybe this will also. I wonder where they will hunt up war next. It is a shame that so many poor men and boys must lose their lives in so cruel a way and I sincerely hope you will come through safely. I really don't know what to write that will interest you. Your letters are so much more interesting. More boys in blue just passed our house on bicycles. I made you a case for your handkerchiefs to keep them together. It is my design which I tried to make to match your cuff box. The violets will remind you of your visit here. I wish you could be here to spend Christmas with us. As usual, we will have a big tree. Mrs. Schneider will decorate the two church hall pillars with white vines and red leaves around them. Oscar will play in the orchestra. He and I practice with the Choral Society and are working on *The Creation* by Haydn. I will let you go with sincere wishes for your safety and happiness.

From your Cousin Rosalie

\*        \*        \*

Dear Cousin Rosalie,
1900

It seems early to think about Christmas but in order to be on time I sent you a few trifles by registered mail. It is very hot here. You will probably be looking for winter clothes now, a thing which a person never need do here in the Philippines. Your season for strolling and picnics in Dubuque will soon be over for the cold season. The other day I saw a number of amateur photographs which received a prize in *LESLIE'S WEEKLY* and one was Dubuque's monument. I assure you that it felt like seeing a picture of an old friend. During the last weeks we had very oppressive heat, but then a typhoon passed over the islands, so at present it is rainy and cooler. We hope it inaugurates the rainy season as that would end the cholera and its many disagreeable consequences; the quarantine, the lack of fresh vegetables and fruit, poor business, etc., not to speak of the deaths. Only thirty or forty Americans have died from cholera, the majority of the victims being natives or Chinamen. The hardships of the campaign plus living in the tropics will run down my system and I'll need to leave. I have not been very well lately, but am getting better. As for happy, can anyone be happy if one loses five good friends within six weeks? You are such a faithful correspondent and I assure you your letters are especially appreciated. With best regards, I remain

Your affectionate Cousin Leo

\*    \*    \*

Miss Rosalie Herrmann
2419 Couler Ave., Dubuque, Iowa

Dear Cousin Leo,

I received the beautiful Christmas present you sent me and thank you very much. I consider myself very lucky to receive a present from so far away. I wear it on my belt and feel very proud as people say, "What a pretty little silk purse you are wearing." Also we enjoyed ourselves so very much over the Philippine (or Mexican?) coins it contained. It is very fuzzy. Papa thanks you for them and placed them in his Museum case. We had a nice tree for Christmas and had quite a time decorating it. Henry and I had that delightful job. We had the tree fastened in the arms of our Santa Claus tree holder and tried to take it into the front parlor when Mr. Santa took a notion to come off his stand. I had to hold tree and Santa while Henry quickly mixed plaster to fasten him in place upright again. About two weeks before Christmas I played St. Nick at my Aunt's house for her two children. I put on a buffalo overcoat and cap, filled a sack with candy, popcorn, and apples, and knocked on their door. The children just looked and looked, but couldn't say a word. After I left they asked all kinds of questions which made the grown-ups laugh. Christmas day was cold. Everyone was glad to stay indoors. In the evening we went to hear the children sing and speak. They received candy, oranges, and nuts. Our church is up two flights of steps from Couler Avenue and hard to reach on snowy days. Oscar sang a part alone. Henry's teacher called on us in the evening and brought Henry his reward of twenty-five pressed flowers from Canada and a picture of Linnaeus. I think I wrote how very much interested Henry is in scientific work. He would be most thankful if you come across any wild flowers if you could press them for him. He would very much like specimens from Manila. He has over two-hundred mounted flowers with leaves and roots. A man came from Alaska bringing with him many specimens of Indian baskets, rugs, and fishing implements. Papa was able to obtain a few. Henry's teacher, who had been in Van Couver Island last summer, brought some Indian baskets, too. You will be surprised to see our collection when you come home on leave. I sent you a postcard with a small view of Dubuque. The view that Papa painted of Sinnapi from Wisconsin is very nice. We have this big picture hanging in our dining room. We all enjoy your descriptions of the Philippines so much. It must be very romantic and so different from here. We will be glad to welcome you when you do come, hoping it will be soon. Thanking you again for your present, I remain,

Your loving Cousin Rosalie

# More Letters from Leo

Executive Bureau, Manila, Philippine Islands

Nov. 1903

Dear Cousin Rosalie,

Gen. Miles and your letter both arrived on the *THOMAS* today. I am sorry to read you have been ill and hope to hear of your speedy recovery. Since my siege of illness I have entered upon a new period of good health and spirits. Since Sept. 20 I have been living at *Nipa Lodge* at Malate. I board there with Mr. and Mrs. Beer in an airy and spacious bamboo house with a nipa roof and porch on three sides, almost all doors and windows without glass or shells, only shutters. The floor is split bamboo about one and a half inches wide with half inch openings between each slat. Pencils, coins, etc., have a tendency to fall through the cracks to under the house where the rigs are kept. Mrs. Beer lost the diamond out of her ring that way and never found it. In consequence of its construction, the house is quite cool. It stands back from the street which was formerly a paddy field.

Every morning I admire the beautiful green fields, graceful tall bamboo, cocoanut, and banana trees, and areca palms, and the huts of the natives from which smoke curls up as little brown women prepare morning fish and rice. Translucent shells found along the sea shore are used for windows almost as they are, needing only to be cut to the proper size.

From *Nipa Lodge* to the *Executive Palace* is a two and a half mile walk which Mr. Beer and I take every morning and evening. At noon we go home to lunch and return in a light rig drawn by a sturdy little pony, Tadco, dubbed thus by his former Chinese owners. We now have several American teachers for neighbors. They have three or four rigs. Our houses are exactly alike, standing twenty yards back from the street and surrounded by high picket fences. Cholera is still on the rampage causing horrible loss of life in the Southern Islands.

The Mexican money I sent you is enough to turn a man's hair gray. Payday one of the boys went to the treasury to cash our checks. He came back with a dozen coolies carrying the money. My pay (328 pesos) must have weighed eighteen or twenty pounds. My opinion of this silver standard is not very favorable when, at month's end, I receive, for a nice little check, a big matting sack full of grimy silver.

General Taft is working hard to give the Filipinos a just and liberal government, but my opinion is they will never be fit to ever think of becoming future citizens of our great republic. As an independent nation, they will be second to Haiti, Liberia, or worse.

I quite like the Philippines in spite of the hard times I've had. My work is pleasant, hours short, and as I am a man of

temperate habits, I am able to save toward a visit home to see my
mother in Germany. Please give my best regards to your parents
and brothers, and receive my best wishes for a Merry Christmas
and a prosperous New Year.


Your affectionate Cousin Leo



                    *        *        *


                                                Manila, P. I., 1903
My dear Cousin Rosalie,


Last night I attended the funeral of Miss Bennett, an American
school teacher and good friend of mine. She was a bright and
enthusiastic worker. First she was stationed in Balanga where I
taught school in 1900, then at Balcolor, then San Fernando, forty
miles from Manila. Physicians have not agreed as to the cause
of death, some saying small pox, or blood poisoning from the
cholera virus. Miss Bennet was best friend of Mrs. Love, wife
of Mr. Love, my best friend. I do not want to stay here to end
up in the cemetery. If I cannot be transferred, I shall leave the
Islands next year and try to find a position in the United States
or Mexico. I may buy a fruit ranch in California. Love and I
intend to go into business together but have made no arrangements so far. I'm not anxious to give up such a well-paid position in the translating department and start anew, but a person
should leave a country whose climate has such a bad effect.

I get up at five or six to exercise and take a long walk on the
shores of Manila Bay, and out to Luneta where I watch the

soldiers drill and natives bathe. In the evening I often stroll on the cool beach. Night is beautiful on the Malecon and Luneta, and I often wish you could see all this. Yet I would prefer to stroll through the countryside of Dubuque with you, in spite of the beauty of the tropics. It is getting dark in the office, and I must go for my evening walk before dinner. I shall therefore close this letter and await your reply.

With best regards, your affectionate Cousin Leo

\*　　\*　　\*

Off the Japanese Coast, June, 1903

Dear Cousin Rosalie,

The *Siberia* is sailing along merrily in the teeth of a fresh breeze, and I will reach Kobe tomorrow. When we arrived in Yokahama early yesterday morning at nine, I went ashore with three other passengers. Yokahama is built along the hills bordering Tokyo Bay as high as the bluffs of Dubuque. The Japanese part of the town has little wooden, oil-papered, tile-roofed houses containing dainty little shops or dwelling rooms partitioned off by sliding oil-papered walls. White people mostly have residences on the bluffs. Sturdy Japanese coolies pulled us around in jinrickishas for two hours. Then we boarded a funny little train for Tokyo. We entered the first class carriage, the seats of which ran the entire length on each side like a streetcar. After Yokahama we passed by swampy rice fields, every inch cultivated, then orchards and truck gardens, then villages and towns of tiny tile or grass-roofed houses. At every stop there was a lively pitter-patter of wooden clogs worn by the Japanese. They wear kimonos and crowd in and out laughing and chattering. In our first class car there were only white people. When we arrived in the capital, Tokyo, we went to a European restaurant for luncheon, then rode jinrickishas past modern public buildings, through parks, past huge walls and moats, through queer gates, and to the foot of a steep hill. We climbed a flight of several hundred steps reaching a hilltop from which we obtained a beautiful view of Tokyo. It lay below, a city of two million people. The view was the same when you took me up the elevator there.

We visited *Showa's Temple* next. How I wish you could have been with me and seen the thousand interesting things I saw! We had to put on overshoes in order to not ruin the polished floors and mats. The temple contained most beautiful wood carvings (camphor wood, or gilt or painted) and bronze work, all sorts of holy drums and gongs. Graves and monuments of all the *Shoguns* and several hundred *Daimas* (petty chiefs) crowd the extensive temple grounds. We saw hanging in another temple yard an oblong temple bell rung by a huge piece of timber shod with iron and suspended beside it like a battering ram. We visited an immense bazaar where one can see and buy, if one has the cash, the most beautiful things imaginable. The Japanese dollar is worth our fifty cents, though it has fifty sens. When we left Tokyo at six p.m. several tough-looking officers of a Russian man-of-war rode in our car. We left Yokahama this morning at ten and are nearing the coast. In the distance we can distinguish

*Fujiyama,* the famous Sacred Japanese Mountain. Give my best
love to your family and favor me with a letter.

Your loving Cousin Leo

\*     \*     \*

Formosa Strait, June 1903

Here is the continuation of my letter. We arrived in Kobe situated beneath high timber-covered hills. After a jinrickisha ride
through town, we went to *Nunobiki Waterfall,* left our vehicles
and climbed up well-kept roads, past a tiny spring in whose
rocky basin swam a number of goldfish, until we reached the
falls. Water falls from a considerable height in a rill it hollowed out of the granite hillside into a rocky basin below. This
is shut off by a high artificial granite wall over which the water
flows like a silvery veil into a seething cauldron below that and
flowing off through a narrow canyon. Surrounded by bushes,
grasses, and flowers, the water is emerald green changing into
silver as it strikes below. A quaint little Japanese inn built on
a bridge spanning the canyon completes this romantic picture.
We visited another waterfall whose fragrant pines reminded
me of the forests of Thuringia. I picked a few flowers, which I
sent you from Hong Kong in a book containing pictures of the
Japanese army, which I bought in Kobe.

The next visit we (three young men, a young German lady,
and I) made to a *Satsuma Ware* factory where four or five men
were painting the most exquisite miniature designs on dainty

vases, teapots, etc. The proprietor said these go through a furnace four to seven times before ready for sale. Genuine *Satsuma
Ware* is very expensive, a tiny vase or bowl costing from ten to a
hundred yen ($5 to $50). We went through temples and bazaars
and the aquarium at *Nanko Temple.* One would not believe the
collection of fish, more like butterflies in richness and varieties of
delicate colors. At five we re-boarded our ship. For scenery, the
wonderful *Inland Sea* of Japan is a mass of all-sized islands, timber-covered, studded with idyllic hamlets and villages. Flotillas
of fishing boats, junks and schooners passed continually. The
*Strait of Shimonoseki* is a half mile wide, a beautiful panorama.
At Nagasaki I went ashore for tea in a Japanese teahouse. They
made us take off our shoes and sit upon floor cushions. There are
too many saloons in Nagasaki and other places aiming to separate a sailor from his hard-earned money. In the evening we
sailed to the shore of the Whangpo and anchored to await high
tide in the night. Next came Woosung, and eighteen miles farther on, Shanghai, the European part being full of beautiful public buildings. The Chinese part is dirty and evil-smelling.

The *Bund* is a fine promenade along the waterfront. Four or
five Chinese at a time patronize a queer wheelbarrow pushed by
a husky Chinaman. Between Woosung and Shanghai, the banks
of the Whangpo are low and flat built up from river sediment,
only fit for grazing water buffaloes. I took a room in the Hong
Kong Hotel. It was so very hot, I couldn't sleep. After four days,
I was glad to leave the place.

After this trip on the *Siberia* I sailed for Manila on the *Rohilla
Marn,* a heaving passage. I was glad to get back to dear old
Manila though the rainy season is late and it's hot. The fire trees

are blooming and the mangoes in season, the finest fruit we have over here. My chief clerk gave me the pleasant tidings that I now will be drawing $150 per month. All were glad I was back at work taking up my share of the burden. I'm now boarding at the Universal Hotel as my friend, Beer, left *Nipa Lodge* and it is not convenient for me to live there. Now, my dear Rosalie, be sure to write to me how you are getting along, and how everybody in Dubuque is. I am so glad to have met you and hope we will see more of each other. With best love to your brothers and parents, I remain,

Your affectionate Cousin Leo

\*       \*       \*

Manila, P. I., 1903

Dearest Cousin Rosalie,

Your last letter was received with pleasure. I should like to be in Dubuque and give you a verbal account of the interesting sights and things I have seen. What a pity that we must resort to speech or even pen to communicate our thoughts and impressions! All is lost before it is understood, it seems. Sunday I was at a funeral of one of my friends who was a Mason and used to work at our office. He was an officer on General MacArthur's staff. We buried him in the National Cemetery at Pasay near Manila. While we were holding the last rites, facing the beautiful Bay of Manila, the meadows, fields, and bamboo groves, millions of grasshoppers were covering the sky like a cloud of smoke. These insects have destroyed nearly all the rice fields in the Philippines. The Government has imported shiploads of rice to check the famine in the provinces. Agriculture is in bad shape as about ninety-five percent of the carabaos have been killed off by rinderpest and locusts, worms, and drought. Cholera is still prevalent in the provinces. Robbers (insurgents, as they call themselves) loot towns and make life a burden to other inhabitants. About one thousand of these outlaws are concentrated in Laguna Province, keeping the Constabulary busy. Governor Taft will leave soon and Wright will take his place. I'm glad, as Taft, although well meaning, has been wrong in his policy of giving the natives *taffy* instead of the firm and just government they need. I often feel as if I should like to be out fighting the *ladrones* (robbers) as life in Manila is becoming rather dull. I love excitement and change, but am old enough to realize it is wisest for me to hold onto my present position. I take great pleasure in remembering my visit with you and I assure you I felt more at home there than at home. I hope we all meet again sometime not too far away and renew our acquaintance. In the meantime believe me that my thoughts often wander to Dubuque. Now, dear Rosalie, I want you to be good and write. Give your parents and brothers my best love.

Your affectionate Cousin Leo

# Cousin Leo's Last Letter

"HERE SHE COMES! Everyone act cheerful," said Mama Lina smoothing her long apron down over her black wool long-sleeved dress. "Only not too cheerful." The family listened as daughter Rosalie slowly descended the hall stairs. Papa Richard wearing business pants, vest, and white shirt, but with his morning breakfast jacket on top, opened the hall door.

"Here's our Rosalie. Come to breakfast, dear." Brother Arthur pulled out the heavy leather-cushioned, brass-knobbed chair for Rosalie. Oscar led her solicitously by the elbow to the table. Young Henry blew her a kiss. Mama quickly poured steaming coffee for her. They searched for any flicker of expression on her face. Soundlessly she sat, automatically placing napkin on lap, unfocused eyes staring just beyond her family's shoulders.

Mama Lina had learned through a long depressing year that appeals to the senses could often bring Rosalie back to reality. Lina lifted the fragrant coffee cup to Rosalie's nose and a slight smile grew on her daughter's lips as she took the cup in both hands like a mug, sipping coffee.

"Good morning, Mama. Good morning, Papa, and everybody.

Breakfast smells good." Lina usually cooked oatmeal and toast, but this day before Christmas she had fried eggs and bacon to brighten Rosalie's spirits. So much to do with so little help! Only a neighbor girl came in briefly each morning to help empty chamber pots.

After breakfast Papa and the boys donned jackets and hurried off to the Dubuque Cabinet Makers Factory on 10th and Jackson. Although high school vacation started today, the factory only closed Christmas Eve. Papa's chief joy as paymaster was passing out the silver dollars with which the men were paid, while his boy Arthur helped with delivery, Oscar running tool machines, and Henry polishing, taking messages, lifting or carrying. In the German tradition, after 8th grade Rosalie had been kept home to help Mama keep house while the boys completed high school. Rosalie worked right beside Lina with the cleaning, cooking, baking, gardening, canning, laundry and sewing.

This past year Lina had found Rosalie worse than useless, staring into space, forgetting to close doors and do chores, not hearing or answering. What could be wrong with her? Should she buy her daughter some Vimont, "the Perfect Health Tonic," sold by DBQ Brewing and Malting Co. out on 32nd and Jackson? No, for deep down she knew what really ailed her daughter. This past year they'd worn mourning since Grandmother and Grandfather Jungk had passed away. It had been fun for Rosalie helping to arrange an apartment for them at the top of the hall stairs and facing the back street with a little private porch looking out on the garden and the carriage and horse barn, then helping move them here from Christian Jungk's farm homestead on the corner of 32nd (and present North Grandview). But they had died. Now the mourning period was over and they could once again don color to celebrate the Christmas season.

If only Cousin Leo and his new wife hadn't paid a visit last Christmas on their return trip to the Philippines. That had compounded the trauma for Rosalie, who'd spent three years writing devotedly to Cousin Leo, her young relative, a U.S. Army Officer serving in the Philippines in the Spanish American War. She'd adored his return letters relating his adventures and travels into Japan and China, his promotion to Foreign Service Translator in the Executive Offices in Manila. Suddenly Leo had walked in their front door, stood beside their Christmas tree, and introduced her.

"Meet my new wife, Mrs. Fischer. She's a widowed relative with two daughters. I met her on my visit home to my mother in Germany. She's been teaching languages in the University in Belgium. We have so much in common. She's endured enough from war. We're leaving the girls with family in Europe for their education. I'm taking her back to the Philippines where we'll start our new life together and both teach in Manila."

Rosalie's face drained of color, her nose pinched white, her lips a stiff thin line, eyes wide. Suddenly she spun away, slammed the door and flew upstairs. She bounded onto the pillows of her bed, knelt there grabbing the brass railing and silently leaned over to pound her head against the wall. Finally she sank down still clinging to the head rails like a drowning sailor. Long after Leo and his wife had finished their visit and gone, Lina found Rosalie there and tucked her under the covers. Rosalie had never been herself since, except when she'd bend over the hot oven to take out bread, or when she'd pump icy cold water from the cistern, or when she'd smell fresh flowers, or eat tasty sweet or sour foods. Lina took to simmering cinnamon and cloves in apple cider at the back of their cast iron stove. She burned beeswax and lavender candles in the parlor hoping to draw Rosalie out of her dense fog. Now Christmas was here again. How would Rosalie endure it?

"Come measure the spices for the gingerbread cookies, Rosalie," said Mama. "We have to bake these for the children's Christmas Eve Program at church tonight."

"Nutmeg and ginger smell the best of all," Rosalie replied as she measured a spoonful of each into the flour mix.

"This afternoon," continued Mama, "I want you to put on your new red and green plaid satin dress with the white ruffled yoke and high color we made from goods we bought last summer at *Ruprecht Bros. Wholesale*. Oscar will take you and Henry to *Immanuelskirsche* in the carriage but he's going to escort Miss Bertha Heckman home after the program so you may have to walk home or take the streetcar. Arthur, as bellringer, will run down early and stay late to open and close."

"Oscar wanted snow so he could drive the sleigh, but at least Arthur's lucky not having to shovel the church steps," observed Rosalie. Their one-horse carriage and 2-seater sleigh with the front bent-knee runners were both made by *Cooper Wagon Works*, as were their bicycles. The slight drizzle of rain seemed to seep through the window and steep Rosalie once more in fog. Listlessly she changed clothes. Something was wrong with her world but she didn't know why. She was caught inside a hollow drum. People on the outside sought attention in faraway muffled shouts and beatings. The pounding in her head drowned them out. Vaguely she noticed perspectives had gone awry. Hallways stretched endlessly. She was so tired. Doorways were too impossibly narrow to pass through at the bottoms, yet their tops slanted out unreasonably wide. Rooms themselves appeared tilted a bit sideways. She'd have to figure it out some other time.

Henry was taking the basket of cookies out to the carriage, so Rosalie followed. Oscar delighted in skillfully driving his blinkered horse and carriage down Couler Avenue. Dubuque at the turn of the century was in rapid change. Power lines were already strung from several tall poles along the edge of each block, but there were still hitching posts in front of every store and dwelling. High stone curbs had been laid. Some boardwalks were already replaced with cement sidewalks. Bricks had been laid on many of the clay streets and new railway tracks for electric streetcars were embedded along the main streets. Oscar stopped his horse carriage at the corner of 24th to look for electric streetcars entering or emerging from the *Key City Electric Car Barn* (which became after one year *Dubuque Light and Traction Rail Co.*) Many of the city's side streets had hand-lit lampposts, but here Couler Avenue was lit by electric arc lamps with cone-shaped metal shades which could be lowered for servicing. Crossing over the rails, Oscar drove on down Couler Avenue past 22nd, to a place called Eagle Point Drive (now Kaufmann Avenue.) The name had to be changed when the Rail Company chose 20th Street to lay their tracks to Eagle Point Park. Their Central Line, which came from South Dubuque up Clay Street, jogged slightly at 18th into Couler Avenue. To Rosalie swathed in her personal gloom, the drive was a murky blur. The front of her mind kept repeating, "I'll get over this," while the back of her mind was screaming, "I'll never get over this. He doesn't love me, he never loved me. I have nobody to love."

Oscar hitched the horse at the 18th Street Firehouse curb and helped Rosalie alight. *Immanuel German Congregational Church* was up two flights of steps on the first terrace above the firehouse. It was a white vertical plank square building with slant roof trimmed with curlicues, even on the bell tower roof. The shutters had been opened to reveal glowing lanterns in the Gothic, arched to a center point, windows three on each side of the building. Rosalie didn't notice the beckoning light. Arthur had climbed the bell tower stairs, lighted by only one small hexagonal window. Rosalie didn't hear his welcoming chime. The Reverend Lyerlie and wife with Baby Betty had come down one flight of steps from their parsonage tucked onto the terrace above the church but one flight of steps up to Seminary Hill. The Christmas program was a distant hum.

"How silently, how silently the wondrous gift is given." Her brothers in the young men's chorus did have beautiful voices. "As God imparts to human hearts the wonders of His heaven." They were boy soprano, baritone, and bass. "No ear can hear His coming, yet in this world of sin," that world split apart the hollow drum in which Rosalie was trapped! "Where meek souls will receive Him still, the dear Christ enters in." A hush fell in the back of her mind, and the front thought, "I've been so foolish, so sinful, so self-centered. He wasn't supposed to love me. He married the right person, someone who'd suffered, who'd been educated, who could share his love of languages. I'm just Cousin Rosalie." The cloud of gloom climbed off her head, uncurled from her shoulders, and crept away on little cat feet.

"How beautiful you look," said the pastor's wife to her.

"That was the loveliest Christmas Program ever," Rosalie smiled back.

Oscar, eyes a-twinkle with anticipation, was showing the equally fun-loving Miss Bertha down to the carriage. They were a vivacious pair. Henry swung the now empty cookie basket as Rosalie followed him down the steps. The rain had stopped. She glanced back at the church over which a pale moon, surrounded by a rainbow aura, glimmered in the misty sky. "Heavenly," she sighed.

Continuing down, she glanced across 18th street reading MCFARLAND'S DRUGSTORE, APOTHECARY, CHEMIST, CITY DRUG STORE, IMPORTED AND AMERICAN MINERAL WATER, SOAPS, TOILET ARTICLES, PERFUMES, COSMETICS, PAINTS, GLASS, OILS, SURGICAL INSTRUMENTS, CORSETS. "Something for everyone," she laughed.

They headed home past 1895 Couler, Nicholas Jacquinot's double brick house with arched passway through the middle giving delivery wagons access to the back. She smiled at the lights shining through little colored glass panes framing the family front door on the left half. On the right side a double door and storefront windows displayed groceries, provisions, flour, and feeds. "Oh Henry, look at the chubby cheeses!" chuckled Rosalie. Down the intersection she could tell that *Lorenz Laundry* at 1896 Jackson was closed dark for Christmas Eve. Except for *Iowa Dairy* at 2141 Couler, almost every building they passed was storefront with living quarters above. Bells and ribbons decorated the barbershops and stores. *P. Jungk's Bakery* across the street at 22nd was busy selling Christmas treats to last-minute shoppers. Spicy baked pfeffernuss fragrance wafted from the opening door.

"Henry, see the row of gingerbread men lined up along the glass looking at us!" From varying lengths of ribbon were suspended pink and green Deutch Letters, cookie dough folded into alphabet or pretzel shapes. There also hung apples studded with whole cloves, which could be used to flavor your hot cider. Henry was most eager to get home where he knew his parents were decorating the tree, and he wanted to help.

On 23rd *Demkier Bros. Straw Hats, Brooms, and Baskets* was closed for the night. Side streets had gas lamps, but with Couler's new lighting you could see all the way to the *Heim Hotel* and the brickyard. At 24th the corner store sign was slanted toward both streets advertising *Mixed Paints, Oils, Watercolors.* Short ramps at ends of each block made walking up onto the sidewalk easier for ladies in their long skirts and high-heeled boots.

Papa Richard was trimming the tree while Mama Lina, in long purple worsted gown, was seated at her piano. It was a square grand piano bought in 1900 when the widowed Mrs. Mary Strueber Renier procured the first pianos in Dubuque and held a sale. Breathlessly Rosalie and Henry burst into the hall calling, "We're home!" Just then Oscar and his girlfriend crowded after them.

"I want to show Bertha our tree!" shouted Oscar.

"The first snowflakes fell! We'll have snow for Christmas after all," Arthur announced, arriving on their coattails. Silence fell as they all at once spotted the white envelope on the lamplit green baize table cover. Everyone watched as Rosalie calmly approached the table.

"A letter from Cousin Leo?"

"Yes," said Mama and Papa softly.

"Shall I read it aloud?" asked Rosalie sitting at the table.

"Dear Mrs. Herrmann, Your Cousin Leo and I send you and your family warm Christmas Greetings. We have warm to spare. Leo is quite used to this heat, and the flies, and the sicknesses which abound, but I am still not acclimated. The little brown Filipinos still seem strange to me, but as so many Chinese, Japanese, Indian, and others have crowded in here, we must all seem strange. I teach all day and Leo teaches after work, so we're too busy to do much else but stroll along the moonlit beaches late evenings. Leo has written dictionaries of three of the islands dialects, which helps the diplomatic executive office run more smoothly. They are sending him on a diplomatic mission to Zanzibar and the Spice Islands next spring. I am looking forward to going with him, although that "traveling companion" Mrs. Love brought him several years ago offered to accompany him. I admit she's handy with needle and brush but she'll just have to stay here and tend to the house and garden. Besides a mule to draw our rig, we have several chickens and pigs. We grow peas, corn, and squash, besides our papayas, guavas, mangoes, and bananas. Tomatoes and potatoes won't grow here. That Spanish friend of his, Pepita, won't be inclined to come and bathe and lounge about while we're gone. They passed a law here the Filipinos can't go naked above the waist anymore, but the women choose such airy see-through cloth for their blouses that it doesn't help much. Leo says General Aguinaldo, whom he thought of as an outlaw, will soon be the elected President. Aguinaldo used the secrecy of the local Masonic Lodge to force rebels into his insurgency. The Catholic Friars have tried to stamp out this very secret organization, but for a different reason. We are sending you some colorful lacquered parasols and woven straw sandals although they are so small probably only children could wear them. With our sincerest regards for your very best health at this holiday season, Mrs. Leo Fischer."

"What a different sort of life," Rosalie laughed shaking her head.

"Are you all right, dear?" Papa asked taking her hands.

"Yes, Papa," she answered kissing his whiskered cheek. "I think when spring comes I'll start raising tropical fish."

"I could make you an aquarium," piped up Arthur.

"Maybe I could raise canaries," mused Rosalie.

"Well, I could build you a screened cage with perches. You could even put a tea strainer in the corner for a nest for their eggs," enthused Henry.

"Or should I cultivate African violets?"

"Let me make a metal tray fitted to the window sill," offered Oscar. "We could put in a layer of pebbles beneath your pots for good drainage."

"No, what I'll do first is start going to the boy's club down on Elm to teach handcrafts and kites, gardening and such." She looked fondly at her brothers. "We've done so many things together, I'll have lots to teach them."

Said Papa," Our Christmas Rose is really back!"

# Father Marquette's First Mass to the Indians

## *At the Mississippi and Fox River Junction 1673*

LOVE, LIGHT, LIFE is our Father, the earth is our Mother, and Jesus Christ brother to man. In the surge of the ocean, in star-swinging motion, we feel the pulse of our God. We sense Holy Spirit compelling us near it; God's hand lifting man from the sod.

Every man on this earth from the advent of birth 'til the moment infinity calls, searching petal division or vast cosmic vision, can find no flaws in God's laws. And to show man his place in harmonious space, Jesus teaches a method and cause.

Love's God's law in the plan for the family of man, mothers teaching it first to their own. Every father must nurture the good gifts of earth, elders echo God's love in the home. Every child must burst forth with the joy song of life 'til we learn the celestial tone.

Stand erect in God's image. Prevent bloody scrimmage. Teach, build, plan, sow, reap for the world. Stretch the brotherly hand round the great global span. Lead man up from his long dismal plod. When the whole human race lifts love's eyes to the skies, we'll reflect back the face of our God.

# In the Case of Lelah-Puc-Ka-Chee

"QUIET IN THE courtroom!" shouted the sheriff over the bedlam of whites and Indians young and old all wanting to be heard. "Court is now in session." Three U.S. District Court judges entered the court for this Northern District of Iowa session. Judge O.P. Shiras towered above them. One look silenced the crowd. His erect figure, grim but spiritual face, his shaggy brows and full crown of hair, his high-heeled top boots, his flowing black silk tie, clay-blue worsted cutaway suit, his vest half buttoned disclosing the expensive white shirt bosom and braid of gold watch chain, all suggested his importance. Judge Shiras had a reputation for deep-rooted principles, thoughtful and honorable judgments, and unassailable convictions. It was his turn to write the decision, but all three judges would decide this case.

"Who comes before this court?" asked Judge Smith.

"Your honor," stammered the sheriff, "this here Indian boy, Ta-Ta-Pa-Cha, has a Writ of Habeas Corpus he wants enforced against this Indian Agent M.J. Malin, but I don't even know where to seat them." He had plucked both from out the crowd and was holding them apart.

"Seat Indians on the right and whites on the left," said Judge Jones.

"That won't work, your honor!" shouted Agent Malin. "These Indian children are wards of mine and should sit beside me because I'm their guardian."

"And by me!" called out School Superintendent Nellis, beginning to possessively herd the Indian children to the left.

"Who speaks for Agent Malin?" Judge Shiras called out.

"I do, your honor, United States Attorney for Mr. Malin."

"And did you appoint Agent Malin as guardian for these children?"

"No, sir, Agent Malin had himself appointed by the District Court of Tama, Iowa, where three years ago a school was built just for them outside their Indian lands."

Judge Smith gave them a piercing stare, finally saying, "Seat the Indian children across the back of the room. The agent and superintendent, and attorney on the left, Ta-Ta-Pa-Cha and the Indians on the right."

"Who speaks for Ta-Ta-Pa-Cha?" called the second judge.

"We do, your honor, Lawyer Jacob Lamb and Tribal Interpreter Joseph Tesson." One was white and the other half-breed, but they sat next to Ta-Ta-Pa-Cha.

Judge Jones raised an eyebrow at a noticeably Indian man seated with the whites. Up he popped explaining, "Your honor, I teach languages with the rest of these teachers." By now the rest of the crowd of onlookers had sorted themselves out on white or Indian sides.

"Let this case proceed," called out the first judge, observing the stony silence and wary but patient wooden-faced Indians. In among the children, Lelah-Puc-Ka-Chee stood out, as she was just blossoming into lovely young womanhood. The students, thirteen girls and five boys, ranging in age from twelve down to four, had all been dressed in sturdy new brown shoes, dark skirts or trousers, and light blue shirts or blouses. All their hair had been cut in short bobs to just below the ears. Upon each girl's head a big light blue bow had seemingly been plastered. Heroic efforts to make them look white had not prevailed against their swarthier complexions, dejected shoulders, downcast eyes, and discomfiture at the hard benches.

Vanity and smugness marked the white group on the left, looking down upon the Indians, whispering and tittering as they straightened their fancy hats and patted their frilly and costly clothing. Like Agent Malin, the white men stretched out their boots, relaxing in their chairs. They owned the place.

Flies crept across the bubbly bluish window glass, sunlight inching across the wooden plank floor. The courtroom was stuffy, Lelah's thoughts were floating free on far-off cool winds, dancing through hushed pines and tall grass, her heart singing, *Feathers and moonbeams, shadows and pale dreams, why stand I breathlessly waiting, for whom? Can I trace in some familiar face a new mysterious spark? Do I hear a strange wild rhythm coming to me from afar? Only yesterday I swung upon the hickory bough. Only yesterday I loved to play at hide-and-seek, to chase the birds, the squirrels, the bees, the butterflies. Now strangers for feelings, searching for meanings. Pebbles rippling water rings, show me my love. Feel his magic pull as I yield to the iron of his embrace. Melt my frozen heart with summer's fire, his lips upon my face. Only yesterday I loved to hear my father's tales. Only yesterday my mother's lullaby rang true, but now it jangles false. There's a passion impatiently pounding. Feathers and moonbeams, shadows and pale dreams, Why sit I breathlessly? Where, oh when, oh what is love?* Suddenly Lelah-Puc-Ka-Chee came to at the sight of her husband, Ta-Ta-Pa-Cha, bravely standing up to the judges, looking them right in the eye, something an Indian doesn't usually do.

Ta-Ta-Pa-Cha's shoulders were broad, his arms strong from doing a man's work hewing logs to fence their Indian lands. He was as tall as Joseph Tesson. Ta-Ta and Lelah had been playmates, had swum the river, herded deer, hunted berries together, always knowing they would someday be married. Now that Lelah was a woman, she'd spent three days alone in the woods as was the tribal rule. Ta-Ta had brought her mother nine pheasants, a basket of seed corn, and a pot of fresh minnows to show he could provide for Lelah.

Mother accepting the gifts made them man and wife. According to taboo, no more could Ta-Ta ever again look upon the face of his mother-in-law, or even be near to her. (Was this Indian taboo meant to prevent interfering mothers-in-law from breaking up a marriage?)

But Agent Malin had seen the lovely maiden alone in the woods dancing, and had enticed her into his carriage with a pretty lace handkerchief and some blue beads. Luring her into his room with his suave smile and seductive eyes, Malin began taking off his shirt. Lelah lowered her eyes from his fascinating curly haired mustache to his hairy white chest and arms, scrawny as sticks. He was *old*, she suddenly realized, and escaped through the door, running like a deer for home.

Furious at being thwarted, Agent Malin next day enlisted Superintendent Nellis to go to the Indian village with him, round up all the Indian children, and take them to school against their will. Iowa law was on their side as it required all underage children to get schooling. Ta-Ta-Pa-Cha had run away the minute they approached him with their gleaming sharp shears to cut off his long braid. With the help of Joseph Tesson, Ta-Ta persuaded Lawyer Lamb to prepare a Writ of Habeas Corpus so the courts would release his wife, Lelah-Puc-Ka-Chee, from school back to him and his tribe.

"Why should she be taken out of school?' asked Judge Smith.

"Your honor," spoke up Lawyer Lamb, "All the tribe, the Chief, and parents feel the school is trying to make their children into whites." The tribe rose as one, nodded silently, and sat down.

"You want her back on a reservation?" asked Judge Jones.

"No, your honor, there is no reservation," explained Lawyer Lamb. "The Tama Indians ceded their lands to the government and were moved to the North West Indian Territory for $800,000 to be paid to them as an annuity according to an 1842 treaty signed with President William Henry Harrison. They returned to Iowa fifteen years later in spite of losing their annuity and bought 80 acres near Toledo and Benton. Then they bought 800,000 acres more. It's private land held in common by the tribe and parceled out for farming. They also have a herd of white deer. They're self-governing, their council choosing as chief whoever has the most years of experience and wisdom, so long as he's effective. They're self-supporting, no poverty, no jails."

"Why did they come back to Iowa?" asked Judge Shiras.

Interpreter Tesson stood, but the Chief stood and gently motioned him to sit. He could speak for himself and his people.

"West dry as dust. No good for corn or deer. Iowa so wide the sky, so cool the breeze, eagles flying over the trees. Pines fold the hills, waves stroke the shore. This the land we longing for, the homing spot for which we yearn. Wherever we go, we shall return. Like coming home to ma and pa. We are at home. This Iowa." There was a lengthy hush in the courtroom.

"Who speaks for Agent Malin?" called out Judge Smith.

"U. S. Attorney McMillan, your honor. We had hoped withholding their annuity would lure them back to the reservation, but 495 Indians are staying in Iowa. An Indian Agents Association was formed to better their conditions. Government could best control this, so the Iowa Legislature in 1896 ceded all Iowa's claims of right or authority over Indians to the federal government under the Department of the Interior. Each Indian gets $45 annually regardless of age or sex. Agent Malin handles this."

"The court calls Agent Malin. To whom do you pay the children's money?" Agent Malin arose but pulled Superintendent Nellis up beside him.

"I pay it to the schools for their room and board. Let the Superintendent tell you about his school."

Nellis turned red-faced, but spoke up. "An appropriation of $35,000 was made and we built this large brick school with laundry building, shops, poultry department, icehouses and root cellar. Boys are taught common education, agriculture, and trades, while girls are taught cooking, sewing, laundry, poultry raising, dairying, and other things a woman should learn. Our teachers are white but we do have one Indian teacher." Nellis looked at his cohort and the possibility of mishandling Indian funds was obvious to everyone in the courtroom. They sat.

The judges called for a one-hour recess while they made their decision.

All three judges returned and Judge Shiras read the opinion. He censured Mr. Malin severely as a self-seeking, self-appointed agent who might be guilty of leading Indian girls astray and robbing Indian men. He said, "Indians are a nation within a nation. Article One, Section Eight of the Constitution says, "The privilege of Habeas Corpus shall not be suspended." Therefore Malin shall release Lelah-Puc-Ka-Chee. Article Two, Section Two states, "Only the President, with advice and consent of the Senate, can make treaties with nations." Therefore District Courts have no jurisdiction to appoint guardians, impose requirements, or force attendance at schools outside the reservations. Iowa no longer has any authority. Agents are only liaisons between the Indian Nation and the federal government. If they interfere there are federal statutes for imposing $1,000 fines. They should be appointed by Department of Indian Affairs, should adopt methods to gain the confidence and esteem of Indians. Federal rulings state: 'Indian communities are dependent on the U. S. government, and owe no allegiance to any state, and receive no protection from it. It is the duty of the Agent or Superintendent to in so far as possible secure the attendance of children between the ages of one and twenty-one at schools." Do not compel or coerce. Only the Department of the Interior can withhold benefits from parents. Seek to interest them. Show them the government designs only to benefit them.'

In the case of Lelah-Puc-Ka-Chee, if she wishes to leave school she has the right. If, although married, she wishes to remain in school, it is her right. If in fact she is not married to Ta-Ta-Pa-Cha, and her parents desire her to stay in school, they may require her to do so until she is eighteen. Only parents can compel attendance, and no other. Lelah?"

Very quietly she stood and made her way past Malin. The Indian women made room for her and she sat immediately behind her husband. She stared at his black braid and saw his ears rise slightly. She knew a smile had stretched across his face.

Judge Shiras's decision that "Indians are a Nation within a Nation" was a landmark in helping keep the peace by giving Indians dignity and respect needed for self-government, excepting for murder or robbery where federal laws took precedence.

CPSIA information can be obtained at www.ICGtesting.com
Printed in the USA
LVOW041646270312

275003LV00003B/7/P